KILK

FC

TALES

KILKENNY
FOLK
TALES

ANNE FARRELL

ILLUSTRATED BY JASON COOKE

The
History
Press
Ireland

First published 2014

The History Press Ireland
50 City Quay
Dublin 2
Ireland
www.thehistorypress.ie

© Anne Farrell, 2014
Illustrations © Jason Cooke, 2014

The right of Anne Farrell to be identified as the Author
of this work has been asserted in accordance with the
Copyright, Designs and Patents Act 1988.

All rights reserved. No part of this book may be reprinted
or reproduced or utilised in any form or by any electronic,
mechanical or other means, now known or hereafter invented,
including photocopying and recording, or in any information
storage or retrieval system, without the permission in writing
from the Publishers.

British Library Cataloguing in Publication Data.
A catalogue record for this book is available from the British Library.

ISBN 978 1 84588 811 4

Typesetting and origination by The History Press

CONTENTS

ACKNOWLEDGEMENTS

Once again I am deeply indebted to many people for their support and guidance.

I am grateful for my upbringing which was steeped in the old traditions, thanks to my late parents, Patrick and Eileen Kirwan, and their friends. They told the stories and showed us the areas of their origin where possible.

Thanks to the friends and old neighbours who have never forgotten the old yarns and are generous in their shared remembrance.

I thank Liam Murphy, a master storyteller, who gave unstintingly of his time and wisdom.

Aisling Kelly and the staff of Kilkenny Libraries were a huge support and I thank them sincerely for their introductions to other folklorists in the county: Kathleen Laffan, author of *A History of Kilmacow – A South Kilkenny Parish*; Michael Brennan, author of *Dearc Fhearna: Its History and Environs*; Seamus Walsh, author of *In the Shadow of the Mines*; the late Patrick J. Cummins, author of *'Emergency' Air Incidents South East Ireland 1940–1945*; Willie Joe Mealy, folklorist of Clogh; and Mary Anne Vaughan, folklorist from Crosspatrick. Ms Nicky Flynn of Kytelers Inn was generous with her time and information as were Vera Meyler and Kitty O'Brien and many, many others. Thanks also to Jonathan Quinn and the Quinn family in Kilkenny for their help with research.

I am delighted that Kees and Anneke Vogelaar gave the information on Mullinabro and thankful to Lieutenant Larry Scallan, curator of the Visitors' Centre in James Stephen's Barracks who was so generous with his time and military-based stories. It was like finding a treasure throve hitherto unexplored.

A special acknowledgement is due to my kind neighbours Elaine Mullan, Ian McHardy and my daughter Hazel Farrell for their proof reading and advice.

Finally thanks to that grand man who married me, Brendan, and to our family who gave encouragement and space when needed.

INTRODUCTION

The voice I bring to this collection of folk tales is that of a storyteller not an academic or historian. History has, however, a way of rearing its head in the best of stories and I have attempted to be historically correct where possible. These are stories handed down from people for people, however, so I would like each reader who picks up this book to enjoy the voice of the story which echoes for them alone.

The stories from the south of the county were bred into the bones of my siblings and I, and so it was wonderful to find that Mary Ann Vaughan was nurtured by similar tales in Crosspatrick in the northern end of the county, despite a big generational gap between us.

The proliferation of saints in the county gave me problems when deciding which stories I should choose for inclusion in this collection. The long-ago saints had great power and their goodness still lingers in many parts of the county and so if I have not included your favourite saint or holy well I hope you will understand my dilemma.

Stories which are included here range from a time when all creatures could converse, as in the Legend of St Evin and St Moling. Knights, fresh from the Crusades, both wicked and good, roam these pages as they once did the land. We did have knights living here in medieval times but we were so busy surviving one invasion after another that we had little time to think about or know the valiant deeds and protections offered by some good men. We did, however, know all about the cruel and hard-hearted ones. The Legend of Grennan Castle is one I love to tell to keep a balance.

On my travels collecting these stories I spoke with people from every walk of life and regret that I cannot include everything. Many people told me of their favourite legends and their small recollections had a way of blossoming into life between us. In a way this book is keeping the faith with the ancient storytellers and bards. I am passing on these stories to all of you to enjoy and to hand on to the next generation.

During the compilation of this collection I have found friendship and help at every turn. People are indeed wonderful. The journey through the folk tales of the county of Kilkenny has given me great joy and a renewed sense of belonging.

1

THE LEGEND OF GRENNAN CASTLE

The Castle of Grennan was once occupied by a medieval knight who went by the name of Denn. He was, by all accounts, a fair and good man and his family and tenants prospered under his care and protection. In fact, his lady wife loved him dearly and proved her love in a most unusual and spectacular manner.

It seems that the good knight Denn was so busy protecting and getting involved in all aspects of rural life that he conveniently forgot to pay his taxes to the king's men who sat in Dublin, counting the vast funds they were collecting from lowly landowners like Denn.

Well, maybe he forgot or else he hoped that they would forget all about him and his lovely castle in Grennan, after all it was a bit off the beaten track when it came to places of importance. But there is always a clever little maneen somewhere when it comes to keeping tabs on people and what they have. It has ever been so since Cain killed Abel. So, news eventually came to the ears of the king that Denn was remiss in paying his dues to his liege lord.

The liege lord to whom Denn was beholden was none other than Richard II of England. Wouldn't you think he had enough to do over in England without bothering poor Denn? Well indeed, he probably had but he decided to take a break from chasing them and came over to Ireland for a little rest; kings don't get much rest you know, for there is always someone hounding them for this, that or the other. King Richard II was no different, some conniving little revenue collector, hoping to ingratiate himself with him, reminded him continually that his wayward subject, the knight known as Denn who held a castle in Grennan had not paid his respectful dues to his sovereign lord.

It appears that the collector, for good measure, said that Denn was getting too familiar with the mere Irish and was adopting their Irish ways and customs. Worst of all was the possibility that because he was becoming so involved locally he was dressing himself in the style of the Irish.

When the king heard this he was nearly hopping mad with indignation at the perceived slights to his royal person. He declared that he would drop in on Castle Grennan when he was travelling from Waterford to Kilkenny and that he would have Denn's head served to him upon a dish at table in the hall of his own castle of Grennan.

Oh, there were some who were delighted to hear this oath declared and many hoped that they would be given the castle for

themselves once the king had feasted his eyes on the head of Denn. Greed is a terrible curse.

In those times the journey from Waterford to Grennan would have taken much longer than it takes today. The king was always accompanied by a huge retinue. The many nobles who accompanied King Richard wished to impress him with their attentiveness and loyalty. They all dressed up in medieval grandeur of the finest wool and silk and bejewelled leather, but were careful not to show colours above or below their own station. Next, came the knights and squires who would be followed by a great number of archers and men-at-arms. Following along on the heels of this grand parade would be the cooks and servants.

Sure, it was like trying to move a whole village with all the paraphernalia they needed. The progress therefore was always going to be slow and it was no wonder then that a man on horseback with nothing to delay him might reach Grennan Castle long before this expedition drew near. Or indeed maybe the word was just passed from village to village until it reached the knight called Denn.

When the Denn household heard about the king's oath to have their lovely knight's head on a platter there must have been a right hullabaloo. If Denn was now truly a man engaged in the ways of the men of Ossory he probably said more than 'Oh heck'. But his wife, on the other hand, took time to think things through. She was a grand woman, bless her.

Well, while King Richard and his huge retinue rested overnight at Knocktopher there was little rest at Grennan Castle. There were a lot of things to be organised and the lovely lady wife of that much-loved knight was clever as well as beautiful. Hurried orders were given and servants were seen to make many trips to the cellars and kegs were loaded up on several carts and sent off into the dark with specific instructions, which must be followed to the letter for the fate of Grennan depended on it.

When the king's progress continued the following day he was amused to find that every mile of the road on the way to Grennan Castle was marked by patient Grennan servants with butts of rich Spanish wine. Needless to say these were sampled and enjoyed by the whole company and it was not cheap wine either, but the best stock to be found in Grennan's cellars.

King Richard was impressed with the gesture and the obvious good quality of the wine being served at each mile-post and expressed regret that he had uttered the oath about having the head of the good knight Denn. He reminded everyone that even though he had regrets he could not go back on a royal oath, no matter what form of persuasion was used. This worried the wine servers from Grennan but cheered up the king's companions for they all thought they still had a chance to gain possession of the castle.

Well, mile passed upon mile and the king was full of the joys of life and wine when he came to the causeway, which led to the gates of Castle Grennan. There, to his amazement, he found the pathway carpeted with the finest rich velvet and brocade and Denn's lovely lady wife waiting patiently to greet her liege lord. Her courtesy was deep and her eyes grave when they met his, which had lost their merriment at the sight of this lavish and respectful display. Regret for his hasty oath was uppermost in his heart but he walked beside the lady as they went into the banquet hall.

The hall was bedecked with the finest furnishings and the tables piled high with every good food and a plentiful supply of wine. However, the king's eyes were drawn to a large silver covered serving dish which was placed directly in front of the seat which was obviously for him. Did he imagine it or was that red liquid seeping out beneath the lid? The king took his place and the lady Denn allowed a blank seat to remain between herself and her monarch. There were many indrawn breaths as the nobles and king's men noted this. A deep silence suddenly hung over the room. The lady Denn gestured with her hand and a servant reached forward, past the king, and lifted the lid from the silver serving platter.

The king recoiled in horror and anguish and the nobles one and all turned pale at the sight which met their horrified eyes. There, pale and bloodied, rested the head of the good knight Denn and red blood flowed freely around the platter.

With a startled oath the king, who was given to oaths, cried out that he would give a dozen of his knights if Denn could be recalled to life. No sooner had the words echoed around the hall than Denn's lady wife rose and drew aside the table covering directly in front of the startled monarch. There on his knees was the good knight Denn with his head stuck up through a hole in the table and fitted with the silver platter like a collar around his neck.

For a moment the king lost his breath and nobles reached for their weapons in genuine alarm then Richard II, king of all he surveyed, threw back his head and laughed until the tears ran down his cheeks. The nobles subsided sheepishly and soon joined in their liege Lord's merriment.

All was forgiven. The king had indeed been served Denn's head on a platter and now all was in order once again. In the full flush of relief and good wine not only did the king forgive Denn but he gave to him additional lands and honours and stayed in his castle for many days hunting with hawk and hounds in the surrounding lands.

When the king and his huge party finally departed from Castle Grennan, the good knight known as Denn, Lord of Grennan celebrated quietly with his lady wife and household and as they drank to the health of Richard II it was noted that no taxes had been paid nor had the king asked for any.

2

THE LEGEND OF
ST EVIN AND ST MOLING

*Did you know that St Evin is the patron saint of New Ross? I don't think
I ever heard his name mentioned when I was at school. A saint with a
name like that would certainly have been suspect as being an English
saint.*

*There is a story about St Evin which makes me laugh. It is brilliant
and it goes like this.*

In the long ago time when St Moling was living in his own private
monastery just a little south of Graigue, which was later to become
Graiguenamanagh, and St Evin was in charge of the religious affairs
in New Ross, the two holy men often had arguments.

You would expect that they would have been arguing about great
theological questions or ecclesiastical matters but not a bit of it.
The two saints had more than religion on their minds. They had
fishing rights to argue about. Can you imagine how it was with the
two of them? They standing on the banks of the rivers with their
robes fluttering in the breeze, trying to best each other.

Now, you know how the salmon come back to where they were
spawned, so that they may finish their life cycle and spawn again in
the same place? Well, each saint wanted the fish to come up the river
they had nearest to them. Wouldn't you think they were trying to
feed thousands instead of a handful of brethren?

The two rivers, the Nore and the Barrow, meet about a mile up
above New Ross, and this was where the problem arose. The two

saints would, at different times, and sometimes at the same time, command the fish to go up the river they considered to be theirs.

St Moling wanted the fish to go up the River Barrow and St Evin was insistent that they go up the River Nore so he could benefit from their coming and going, for if they spawned in the River Nore then their young would return to that river to spawn eventually, and the same would apply to those who went up the Barrow.

Now, all the fish in both the rivers were becoming increasingly annoyed by the constant commanding and counter-commanding by the holy men. It appears that they would often ban or excommunicate the poor creatures if they didn't do as they commanded. In fact the poor fish, who had no wish at all to offend or upset the holy men, were themselves becoming so weary that they were not even fit to finish their journey to the spawning grounds.

So the fish got together and told the saints that there had to be an end to this constant bickering. In a moment of clarity the two saints agreed that they would be guided by whatever the fish would decide.

A day and time was set when they would all meet at the confluence of the two rivers and there, after holding a Conclave, the fish would listen to both sides and whichever river the fish felt 'in conscience bound' to choose would be the one they would reside in ever after.

Well, the time came for the meeting of all parties. It was a lovely summer morning and St Moling, who had the furthest distance to cover, set out to get to the meeting place. He journeyed all along the banks of the Barrow and, on coming to the arranged place, he found he was early and so sat down in the shelter of a tree to rest while he waited. Now, saints are no different from any of us and, being tired and the sun warm on him and the constant murmur of the rivers meeting, didn't the poor man fall sound asleep.

St Evin, on the other hand, had a short distance to travel from Ross and came to the scene refreshed and relaxed. He looked around for his opponent and soon found him snoring loudly where he slept. Ah ha, thought he and, without a hint of remorse, he went to the water's edge and with great eloquence he addressed the congregation of fish who were waiting to give their judgement. His voice throbbed with sincerity and his arguments seemed entirely reasonable and sound to the listening Court of Fish.

They called for his rival to stand forth and give his position but, of course, the still sleeping St Moling never heard them call his name and, I hate to mention this, but St Evin made no move to wake him either. Sure, the fish in the water didn't even know he was snoring just a few yards away.

When St Moling didn't answer them or appear before them the fish decided that he was being contemptuous of their court and, if he chose to ignore their attempt at justice, then they had no choice but to rule in favour of St Evin, who had given such a marvellous oration in favour of the River Nore.

Their decision was that henceforth the salmon would consider the River Nore to be their parent river, and the lesser trout and all the other fish would frequent the River Barrow.

St Evin rejoiced with them that they had made such a wise decision and waved them on their journey up the River Nore with many blessings in both Latin and Gaeilge. Only then did he approach the sleeping St Moling and wake him up.

St Moling was a bit disconcerted when he realised that he had missed the Conclave of Fish and had been ruled against, but apparently this is where his saintliness finally showed itself, for he accepted their ruling and acknowledged that the joke had been on him.

There are mixed stories about what happened after. Some say that the older salmon who had already gone up the River Barrow continued to spawn there so that St Moling didn't have to suffer the deprivation but it appears he never told St Evin of the defectors.

St Evin and his fellow monks enjoyed their salmon, firm in the belief that St Moling was feasting only on trout.

I said it often before and you will probably agree with me now: 'You never know with saints.'

This legend is mentioned with much more detail and eloquence in Nooks & Corners of the County Kilkenny, *by John G.A. Prim.*

3

DEARC FHEARNA
(THE CAVE OF THE ALDERS)

The tales about Dearc Fhearna are many and varied, depending on who is doing the telling. It was the old name for the Dunmore Caves and that name was on it long before St Patrick or any of the saints passed that way. The more modern name of Dún Mór, which means the big or great fort, really applies to the townland around about rather than the caves themselves and indeed the remains of ring forts are clearly visible close by.

It was known as one of the three darkest places in Ireland. The other two 'dark places' were named as the Caves of Knowth and Slaney. The naming of a place as 'dark' would have had several meanings, even in prehistoric times. It was already known as Dearc Fhearna before the coming of the Vikings so it was not the Viking massacre, recorded in *The Annals of the Four Masters*, in 928, that gave it the name. No, I think it went back to a time when trees and groves of trees held special significance in the everyday lives of our ancestors.

As you and I know, there is a whole separate folklore associated with trees and their significance, so I will just give you what I know about the alder. There are mentions in old manuscripts of 'Tree Judgements' (*Fidbretha*) where every tree had a respected position according to law. There were penalties for damage done to different trees.

The alder was listed as *Aithig fedo* or Commoner of the Wood and if a branch was cut from it there was a fine of one sheep. To cut a fork of the tree brought a fine of a one-year-old heifer, for base felling of an alder, one milch cow and for the total removal, the price of two and a half milch cows. How they managed that I dare not think.

The old folk tales record many sacred sites on which sacred groves existed and were often subject to being attacked and uprooted by rival tribes or clans. This was done in the belief that it would weaken the resident tribe or maybe even oust them altogether. Groves such as those were known as 'bile'. Maybe Dearc Fhearna was named for a sacred Grove of Alders.

I think the cave system was probably created by the earth stirring itself. I would also like to believe that it gave shelter to many creatures while the earth was still young. If the old tales are true then there must have been more than one opening into these underground vaults, and there is a possibility that there may have been many another entrance from the valley of the nearby River Dinin. But you know the earth is restless, and there was ample time for rocks to fall and close off access. Sure, a trickle of water can wear away any stone eventually, and there are many trickles of water still to be found in the depths of the caves.

When people populated this area and found this place they must have been excited and probably a little afraid. Deep dark places could be a cause of terror, for who knew if a creature from another time, or indeed another world, still inhabited it. But when needs must the devil drives, they say, and perhaps the need for shelter or safety drove them into the opening.

Perhaps they came upon the ancestors of the giant cat, named in Broccan's poem in *The Book of Leinster* as Luchtigern (Lord of the mice), but wherever they came into the cave, they more than likely found it to be a safe shelter with fresh water running in a stream in its depths.

There had to be a more convenient way in because, if you look at the steep access which is there today, you will see that it would have been too hard to defend and too wet and dangerous for normal coming and going in winter. In those times, they had druids and people who knew and understood the earth better than we do today, so maybe they could divine for such places.

Michael Brennan, whose father John, God be good to him, was the self-appointed custodian of the caves during his lifetime, told me that he remembered when he was a lad, that there was work going on in a quarry area of the farm, and it was thought that there had been another entrance, maybe even the main entrance, to the caves from that site.

It was from Michael that I got the story about the time when a fox went to ground in the caves as he was being chased by the hounds, and one hound followed him into the underground caverns. Later that day there were reports from people in Kilkenny City, seven miles away, that they could hear the sound of a hound yelping under High Street.

He told a similar tale about the time when some bright sparks decided to send a drummer boy through the caves, and again the sound of drumming was heard under that same street. There are lots of empty spaces under the earth that we know little or nothing about, so maybe the sounds of both hound and drummer boy were echoing through these spaces from somewhere back along the cave system.

I have also heard stories which say these caves were linked through underground ways to Kilkenny City and indeed to the Castle itself.

This particular story is, I believe, a tongue-in-cheek tale which is told about the time when the Jacobites and Williamites harried and fought each other up and down Ireland. The Williamites had no sense as they wore their bright Red Coats which were clearly visible against the countryside. Well, it appears that a squad of Red Coats, fresh out from their barracks in Kilkenny City, were hard on the trail of local rebels and, confident that they had them cornered, they followed them down into the caves.

Mark my words, they would have skiddered and slid down that steep slope, leaving daylight and safety behind them. Their grand red coats must have been destroyed. I expect there were many words said which could never be set down here, as they stumbled and struggled through the rock-strewn cavern. They must have had some form of lighting, perhaps a tar brand or two, to persevere so obstinately with the chase. Perhaps they could hear the sounds of the rebels ahead of them.

Whatever took them deeper and deeper into the dripping wet and black dark caves we will never know, but not one single Red Coat ever came back up out of that wide mouth in the earth.

The story goes that some time later the sound of their fifes and drums were heard coming from underneath Kilkenny Castle. The possibility of the cave being connected to Kilkenny Castle may not be too far-fetched, but there had to have been a way out somewhere in the grounds of the castle. Perhaps it was connected up from the first building of the castle.

Having been down into the caves myself, I cannot see how they would have managed to bring their fifes and drums down, let alone play them. It's unlikely that they had them with them as they chased the rebels. Some people tell terribly questionable stories, don't they?

My guess is that the rebels put paid to the Red Coats but we will never know for sure or, knowing Kilkenny humour, maybe the soldiers came back up but their coats were no longer red.

In the early 1960s I went exploring the Dunmore Caves with my brother Seamus, God be good to him. The caves were still undeveloped, at that time, and when we came to them the cave mouth was partially hidden with scrub and young saplings. Ivy and ferns trailed down overhead. It was into this dark, yawning mouth in the earth and down a steep slanting slope we had to go. We secured a rope to a young tree and let ourselves down into the darkness below.

We had small hand torches and a spare flash-lamp from a bicycle. It was cold but the air was easy to breathe. A length of rope stretched between us, secured around our now cold bodies, in case either of us should slip, and far above us the mouth of the cave seemed to get smaller and smaller.

At the end of the first slope it levelled off for a little bit and then we followed it around to the left. We came upon some odd bits of bone but I thought they must have come from some long-dead animal. The going was not easy and the pool of light from our torches was small indeed. We scrambled over rocks and boulders and our voices echoed eerily as we came out into a high vaulted cavern.

We had no notion that this underground world had already been named by various explorers, who gave each section a title such as the Fairies' Floor, which we had recently crossed, the Market Cross, Haddon Hall, the Cathedral and the Crystal Hall. With the innocence of children, who think their parents know nothing, we journeyed on. Maybe it was just as well that we did not know because each discovery we made was a wonder to us, and our hearts hammered as we made our way into this dark unknown.

It was at this suitably scary point that my brother decided to tell me about the massacre that had occurred in these caves. Apparently this story was recorded in *The Annals of the Four Masters* long ago. The Annals record a devastating attack on a small settlement near to Dearc Fhearna.

The Viking horde had penetrated far inland, and were more than likely heading for the monastic settlements in and around Kilkenny City, where they would have rich pickings. It was probably by chance that they came upon the settlement. Even though this settlement seems to have had maybe two large ring forts and some lesser enclosures, they had little or no warning. It is reported that more than 1,000 people fled to the caves. Perhaps this number is exaggerated, but there was a monastic presence in the nearby Rath of Mothel which probably drew in a local population.

Well, to get back to my story, as you can imagine the trail left by so many people, in full flight, must have been impossible to miss, and so it was that the Vikings came upon the cave entrance, where surely there must have been sounds of terror still echoing on the air.

Vikings were not new to this kind of thing so, without bothering themselves overmuch, they gathered the makings of a good fire from the surrounding woods, filled up the mouth of the cave, and set it alight. With a great number of souls trapped in the deep dark cave, it must have been horrific. Had it been just a small number they might have survived by penetrating deeper into the caves, but a thousand had no chance at all.

As the smoke began to smother them, and hot debris from the fire began to fall down towards them, they had little option but to surrender. Many of them were probably hurt already from the mad scramble down.

It appears that, in an effort to hide or save the women and children, the men went up first. The Lord help them, they were immediately taken captive and hauled away, probably to be traded or used as galley slaves. The women and children would have been an encumbrance to the fighting horde, so they were left with the fires still burning over them. Maybe some were able to get out after the Vikings left and the fire died down. I would like to believe that, and also that the sacrifice of the men was not in vain.

How many lost their lives in the caves is not known for sure, but the recorded remains, which have been found and removed, over the years, account for forty-four people. Nineteen were female adults and twenty-five were children. Perhaps there are still many undiscovered remains, or maybe they did take some of the young women, as slaves, also.

Scrambling along on the heels of my brother I was suddenly aware of how vulnerable we were. What if someone undid the rope we had tied off to take us back up to the surface? Then, in the light of his flash-lamp, my brother picked out the first stalactite and I forgot about everything in my wonder.

It was like nothing I had seen before. He told me how this had dripped and dreeped down through the rocks above until the minerals in the water had hardened over hundreds and thousands of years. There was a nub of another one being formed from the ground up and he told me that it was easy to remember which was which. Stalactites come down and stalagmites come up. His torch light picked out several more formations, and it was impossible to see where some started, as the light seemed to get swallowed up in the deep dark.

A short way further on and his delighted exclamation echoed loud. We were almost on top of a huge formation of calcite. It looked like it had melted down, almost like candle grease from some massive candle high above, out of range of the light. We stayed a long time just looking at this wonder. It was almost sticky to touch, and we both regretted that we had no one else with us to enjoy the spectacle.

Once we knew the stalagmites were there we kept our eyes open and were very careful where we stepped. It was still difficult to get about safely. We climbed up a slanting ridge and found our way through a very tight entrance into another cave beyond. Our lights were of little or no use in the total darkness and the climb down on the far side got more difficult by the minute. There was the constant sound of drips and plops, and even when we shouted loudly our voices seemed to get swallowed up in the vast interior darkness.

The stalactites and stalagmites seemed to be a dirty grey colour, but then we had only small torches. Some looked brittle and spiked down dangerously from above, while the ones beneath our feet seemed squat and nubby.

The possibility that treasure might be hidden there did occur to us, but our means of searching was so limited that we abandoned the thought. The flashlights were small so we decided to return to the surface before our lights gave out.

I will never forget the sensation of coming back up from the chilly damp depths to step into the air over ground. The 'fresh air' stank and took a while to get used to.

We never went back to the cave, and years later we heard that it was being developed by the County Council as an amenity.

Having since read accounts of how other explorers, in Dearc Fearna, found human remains encased in the same glistening grey calcite, and skulls lying in the water of the well, I am very glad we didn't have better light and didn't stumble across them.

Later again we heard that a large hoard of silver and bronze items were found, probably not too far from where we passed. It included silver ingots and pieces, which were dated back to AD 970. These are now in the National Museum.

Wouldn't it have been a grand end to our adventure had we found them that day?

There are tales that tell how Dearc Fhearna has witnessed many strange and historical events, but they are, as far as I can trace, just mentions with no great folklore attached to them. That it was used as a hideaway for rebels in different centuries, and as a place of safety for hedge schoolmasters and priests during our dark periods of history, are probably very true.

I recently came across a lovely ballad, 'The Cave of Dunmore', written by Br Leandor McGrath which includes a lot of these events. It was published in a book called *Dearc Fhearna: Its History & Environs*, written by Michael Brennan, and is reproduced here with his kind permission.

In primeval ages by natural laws
The joints in the limestone developed some flaws,
The water and gases dissolved the limestone,
Till the Cave of Dunmore existed alone.

Go down Mothel lane, cross two fields of White,
Till the mouth of the Cave appears just in sight,
Slide down the steep scree, you've got three ways to go,
You light torch or candle, your guide's bound to know.

For one hundred yards, over rocks great and small,
You stumble and scramble, you slide down and fall,
See stalactites, stalagmites, grown from a cone,
Till at last you arrive at the Fairies' Grand Floor.

In fancy you image the hosts of the Sidhe,
As they dance and make merry, led on by their Ri
But hark you hear echoes, the elk and wild deer,
Pursued by the wolfhound, seek refuge in here.

When Purcell, the Norman, to Ballyfoyle came,
He built a grand castle and killed all the game,
Irish Patriots met in the Cave of Dunmore
To resist the invader of Eire's dear shore.

When Cromwell the women and children gored
In old Irish town on the point of the sword
The Irish resolved in the cave in a band,
His scouts and outriders to slaughter off hand.

The priest and the friar in dark Penal days,
Here offered the Mass the Almighty to praise,
While the faithful remembered the Catacombs cold
Where the first Christians gathered, their rites to unfold.

Volunteers, Peep-O'Day Boys and White boys, also
Crohoore-O' the Billhook and gallant John Doe
Then Fenians, Land Leaguers, Republicans, too,
Made the cave their headquarters, to freedom's cause true.

Dear Cave of Dunmore! How my heart with you thrills,
Your recesses and passages history fills.
For ages and ages you've sheltered a band,
Of true Gaels fired with love for their dear native land.

(Br Leandor McGrath was born in Kilmadum, Ballyfoyle, and along
with two of his brothers, he joined the De La Salle Order. He wrote
a selection of poems known as 'Poems of Ballyfoyle'.)

The wood of the Alder was used to make shields and bowls and other
containers. The bark, the leaves and catkins were used to make dyes.

The leaves of the alder, when placed in your shoes, were said to cool the feet and prevent swelling. In more modern times the wood of the alder has been used in the making of bridges and locks on canals as the timber becomes very dense and hard when left in water.

If you have an interest in geology and caves then you might enjoy that grand book called Dearc Fhearna: Its History & Environs, *written by Michael Brennan from the same area, which gives fascinating details about the caves and wonderful pictures to go with them.*

The Dunmore Caves are now open to the public and a tour guide can take you safely down many, many steps into a cavern where electric lighting shows clearly the hidden wonders beneath the earth. Details are available online at dunmorecaves@opw.ie.

4

Ciarán of Saigir (St Kieran)

Do you know, I have spent a long time pondering a matter of no concern to anyone except myself. It involves how St Kieran's parents came to meet.

When you hear the reason for this strange preoccupation you might even join me in trying to figure out how a grand girl, called Liadán, who was born on the Island of Cape Clear, off the County Cork coast, came to meet with a fine strapping lad from County Kilkenny. His name was Lugna or Laighne and he was a nobleman from Osraige. Lugna was probably the name his own people used every day and 'Laighne' his official name.

Once the thought occurred to me I couldn't leave it alone. I have harried and hounded it in my mind to find an answer and the only conclusion I can come to is that, for some reason, that sensible Kilkenny man found himself caught up in an adventure which took him down through the land of the Deise until he reached the boundary of the sea in county Cork.

By the time he reached the edge of the land he would have met and been in contact with a tribe, known, at that time, as the Corcu Loígde. Liadán was of this tribe. Whether he journeyed out to Cape Clear Island or not I cannot tell but, if I were him, I wouldn't have been satisfied to stand on the shore looking out at the islands. Sure, haven't I made that journey, many a time, to set foot on that same island? Curiosity is a terrible thing. You should think of going there for it is a place to revive your soul.

Well, however it came about, either by accident or arrangement, he finally met the lovely Liadán and they were married. It would have been hard for a girl born so close to the sea to move inland and she must have dreaded it, for it is said that once you are born to the sound of the ocean and the cry of the gulls your heart will long for the sea ever after. I have found this to be true.

It seems that the people then were always on the move and thought nothing of making long journeys. They probably looked on the travelling between places as a grand adventure and took their time about it. Not a bit like today when we are nearly meeting ourselves coming back.

At this time, in Ireland, the druids were still well respected and the first hints of Christianity were coming into the country. St Declan of Ardmore would have been on the move then as would St Ailbe of Emly and many other saints. The newlywed Liadán is said to have consulted with the local druids as a result of a strange dream she had. She dreamed that a star fell from the sky into her mouth.

The poor young girl must have got a fright but the druids interpreted the dream in a way which may have eased her mind. They told her that she would give birth to a son and that his fame and virtues would be known as far as the world's end. She must have been delighted to know she would have a boy as, in tribal matters, it was always important to bear a son.

There is not much information about the months which followed. I expect the young couple went back to Osraige and settled there until near the time for Liadán, to give birth. Like all young girls she wanted to be near her own people at such an occasion and it appears that they made the journey back to Cape Clear. Bless her, I hope the weather was kind to her on her way, but sure, what am I thinking of? She was a strong healthy island born woman.

However, to cut a long story short, she gave birth to her lovely son, Ciarán, within sight and sound of the ocean.

I suppose, like many other families, the young couple and their son were inclined to visit and spend time with both sets of parents. So young Ciarán grew up knowing the countryside of Osraige and the hills and hollows of Cape Clear.

Indeed, if legends are to be relied on, it appears that even in his youth Ciarán had, on the island of Cape Clear, a quiet place where he liked to contemplate, and a blessed well, bearing his name, still exists there.

Some people say that it was through his visits to the island that he discovered Christianity. Others think that it was through his father's people in Osraige that he learned about Christ, for it is rumoured that even before St Patrick took to journeying around Ireland, that other holy men had introduced Christianity in many southern areas.

My own thought on the matter is that the people of the Deise were already well disposed towards St Declan and Christianity. Indeed, his miracles must have been well talked about when people gathered together. This must have had some influence on the young Ciarán, but then sure what do any of us know about that long ago time?

There is a story about Ciarán, in his early days, which tells how he was very compassionate and kindly to everyone, not least the birds and animals around him. It is said that once he was out walking and he saw that grand bird, called a kite, come swooping down to take a little bird straight off its nest. Ciarán was greatly upset and the kite, sensing his distress, turned and brought back the little bird, which was now sorely injured, and dropped it at the young man's feet. He put his hand to it and commanded it to rise and be whole, and the little bird came back to full health and went once more to sit untroubled upon its nest.

You see that is the difference between us and the saints. They never hesitated, but believed absolutely in the power of God working through them.

Sometimes now we are inclined to think that people who lived then were uneducated and wild, but this was not the case at all. Ciarán was well educated and went as far as travelling to Tours in France and then on to Rome to further his education, so dedicated was he to Christianity.

I have heard it said that while he was in Rome he met with St Patrick and they got on well together. In fact, it is related that as he was leaving for Ireland, St Patrick gave to Ciarán instructions to build a monastery at the site of the Well of Uaran. Ciarán thought about all the wells known to him in his homeland and asked the

saint how he would find this particular well. St Patrick gave to him a little bell, and told him that it would not sound until he reached the place in which the monastery was to be built.

Wasn't that a strange thing entirely?

When Ciarán came home from his travels he was terribly holy, by all accounts, and decided to build himself a little small one-room shelter, called a cell, in a place called Saigir, not too far from the Slieve Bloom Mountains.

His parents must have been distracted, the craturs, and all the education he was after getting abroad. But sure, maybe they had other children who were able to follow in their father's footsteps. There is never a mention of a cross word between them anyway. With someone so obviously good and holy what could they say? Little miracles were happening wherever Ciarán went and people loved him.

It seems that other good young men flocked to where Ciarán had his hermitage. He was not going to get any quiet time for hermiting, as they say. In no time at all he realised that he would have to begin teaching and educating these young men. First of all he had to start on making little cells for them, like his own. Now this is where we hear one of the strangest tales about the saint. I am not sure if there is even a grain of truth in it, but I will tell it to you and you can decide for yourself.

The animals were all very attracted to Ciarán because, it is said, he practised his preaching with them, out in the woodlands, and apparently they befriended him. The story goes that while he was helping the young men who had come to join him to build their cells, a fox, a badger and a wolf worked with the men and helped in the building.

One day, the fox, being a rogue by nature, stole Ciarán's shoes, and Ciarán sent the badger to get them back. In no time at all the badger caught the fox and brought back both fox and shoes to the saint. Apparently all Ciarán did was to order the fox to repent for taking the shoes, which was a sin. The fox repented and returned to helping with the work.

I often wonder about this story and think it might be mixed up with the story of how Ciarán decided to move on from Saigir and headed north to Freshford and Johnstown, and on the way he was robbed of all his possessions, even of his sandals. All that was left to him was his cloak and, by some miracle, the little bell, given to him by St Patrick. He still had not found the Well of Uaran or heard the bell sound. But the thieves never found the bell, even though it was with his cloak, and, lo and behold, a few miles further on, as he was crossing a little hill, didn't the bell ring for the very first time. Well, the poor saint must have got the fright of his life. He had been waiting and wondering about the task St Patrick had given him for a long time and now here, all unlooked for, the little bell had sounded.

Ciarán took the bell and hung it on the branch of a nearby tree, and there it continued to sound out its little ringing chimes, all unaided. So there it was that Ciarán rested and began to build what came to be known as the great church of St Ciarán. This place became the chosen burial site for the kings of Ossory.

Before I finish my story I must tell you that St Ciarán's mother, Liadán, is reported to have come, with some female friends, in her later years, to help her son with his work. She must have been worrying about him, and he so taken up with teaching and preaching that he might even forget to eat. The women set up what is now thought to be the first Christian nunnery in Ireland.

St Ciarán was known as one of the Twelve Apostles of Ireland, and many are the miracles attributed to him. Some miracles are to do with bringing back to life those who were mortally wounded in battle. But then most of the saints of that time seemed to have this gift of healing, which set them apart from their fellow men. He lived in a time of great spiritual change, and had the courage to walk his own path.

He is said to be buried in Tullahern in County Kilkenny, and his feast day is 5 March.

5

THE FLYING
FORTRESS

Before I tell this story I wish to acknowledge the kindness and help
I received from the late Patrick J. Cummins. He hailed from the village
of Slieverue, in County Kilkenny, not far from where I grew up and
our parents knew each other from childhood. Paddy Cummins did a
powerful amount of research regarding air incidents in Ireland during
the war years. His book *'Emergency' Air Incidents South-East Ireland
1940–1945* is a mine of information. May his gentle soul rest easy.

A storm had been blowing in from the north-west for some time
before Thomas Henderson went out across the fields. He was looking
down over 'The Park', which was a marshy area but had been successfully
divided into fields by the local farming community. Grangefertgh was
the name given to the townland, and the nearest village was Johnstown,
in the north of County Kilkenny. If you went further north you would
be through Crosspatrick and in the next county before you knew it.

Between the stormy weather and the war it was a worrying time
for everyone. There were shortages of nearly everything and rationing
was now the norm. People were queuing for tea and sugar and it was
not easy to keep families fed and cared for. Ireland was maintaining a
neutral position politically, but they were still short of all the things
which would normally be imported. The rest of the world seemed
intent on killing each other, and there was no obvious end in sight.

Thomas Henderson must have had some of these worries on his
mind that day as he stood in the field on the family farm. As the
storm clouds streamed on the wind he thought he heard something

and looking harder he couldn't believe his eyes. The biggest aircraft he had ever seen was coming down through the clouds, with its engines making a stuttering sound, as though they were cutting in and then out again. Then it seemed to go into a glide and came down low over the fields.

There was no time to think or do anything before the huge aircraft skidded over the grassy surface and was tearing along the field. It tore through a hawthorn hedge, demolished a stone wall and bounced over another hedge that formed the boundaries between the fields in 'The Park'. There was nothing quiet about the landing for as it came down and hurtled through the fields the starboard wing was torn off and the engines were flung hither and yon. The broken wing was tossed up into the air and it came down on the other wing, causing further damage. The fields where it finally came to rest were owned by Mrs Mary Holohan, Mr Nicholson, Michael Duhaney and Gerard Henderson.

Well, the sound of the dying engines and the crash which followed was heard by many and Gerard Henderson, the older brother of Thomas, came hurrying from the family farmstead down across the way. Thomas was sent to Johnstown to fetch a doctor as they were sure there would be some badly injured airmen in the aircraft which was now lying quietly in the fields below. Thomas sped away with his heart hammering, sure that great haste was necessary now to maybe save some lives, for there had to be several people on board such a huge craft.

He alerted the local Gardaí as he went and he quickly returned with Dr Hynes, the local GP, in tow. He was thankful when he returned to see that there was no sign of the aircraft catching fire. Together with the doctor he approached the downed craft and they gained entry. Imagine their astonishment as they called out to the victims, which were surely there, only to be answered by silence and, fearing the worst, they pressed further in only to find the craft empty of all human occupation. How could it be and where were the crew? Was it like the *Marie Celeste*, only of the airborne variety? It would be many hours later before the full story would be known.

In the meantime many of the locals had arrived. Once it was established that no crew were aboard and no one was hurt or deceased the first arrivals had free reign. In a time when everything was rationed it was like finding Aladdin's cave. The huge belly of the aircraft was packed to capacity with ammunition, the crew's personal possessions, uniforms, clothes, tinned food, cigarettes and papers. When the aircraft came down and broke up lots of its contents were scattered through the fields before it came to a halt. For a very short while it was like Christmas had come late. Warm clothing, tinned food and many another useful items, besides. Sure, 'twas like manna from heaven.

The arrival of the Gardaí from Johnstown saw a scattering of civilians as they vanished, with their spoils, back to their own homes in the surrounding area. Nothing else could be removed now that the authorities were on the scene. The Gardaí were aided in their efforts to cordon off the site by the Local Defence Force from Johnstown and Galmoyle. It seems that everyone wanted in on the act for shortly after a detachment of military from Templemore Military Barracks, in Tipperary, arrived. Not very long afterwards they too were replaced by another detachment which came out from the Military Barracks in Kilkenny, as it was in their territory the crash had occurred.

No matter how many arrived none could shed any light on how the aircraft had flown itself or what had happened to the missing crew. No one had seen or heard of anyone bailing out in the surrounding countryside so there were many questions to be answered. The only thing they were sure of was that it was an American Aircraft.

In fact it was one of the newest, best equipped aircraft produced by Boeing for the USA Air Force. It was officially known as B-17G but was named by those who flew her as the Flying Fortress. An account of her specifications given Paddy Cummins reads as follows:

She was equipped with an electrically-powered Bendix 'chin' turret, armed with two 0.50in. M-2 Browning machine-guns, fitted under the nose, improved turbo-superchargers for the engines and other modifications. The B-17G, which could carry up to 13,000lb of bombs, was also equipped with the latest navigation, radio equipment and the top-secret Norden precision bombsite. A defensive armament of thirteen 0.50in machine guns was also installed at six different positions in the aircraft's fuselage. The aircraft normally carried a crew of ten, comprising a pilot, co-pilot, bombardier, navigator (all officers), flight engineer, radio operator and four air gunners (all Sergeants).

Well, with all that equipment available to the Flying Fortress wasn't it a wonder that it now sat with its bottom embedded in the marshy land of The Park? Sure, the locals and officials who attended at the scene in the first few hours had no notion at all of the importance of this aircraft and were mystified as to how it came to be there with not a sinner on board to guide or man her.

The story of this particular Flying Fortress started much earlier that day. She took off from Goose Bay Airfield in Labrador, Canada. She was bound for an airfield near Belfast called Nutts Corner. Her crew included 2nd-Lt Charles G. Smith, Jnr (pilot), Ft-Off. John M. Haning (co-pilot), 2nd-Lts Ralph F. Wise, George Avilles, Jnr, Raymond Niday and Vernon D. Gardner.

The weather conditions were poor from the start and the Flying Fortress by all accounts 'went on instruments' almost immediately after take-off and had to climb 13,500 feet to avoid ice collecting on the wings. They had none of the fancy sprays which they can use now to de-ice the wings. Most of the journey was uneventful and they took radio bearings from beacons on the coasts of Greenland, Iceland and later on from Ireland. These supplied navigational 'fixes' during the flight eastwards so they knew they were on the right flight path to take them to the small airfield at Nutts Corner, in Northern Ireland. This was important because the Republic of Ireland was, of course, neutral and they couldn't be landing there, now could they?

When they were approximately 200 miles off the Irish coast they had to climb again to get over the storm clouds which stretched ahead. The first hint of trouble came when the No. 1 engine began to run rough. Not too far more and the No. 4 engine had to be cut out. By now they were over land and the pilot was beginning to bring her down through breaks in the cloud cover. They had come over a small airfield known as St Angelo, in the County Fermanagh, when the No. 3 engine started running rough also. They were decreasing the power rapidly now and hoped to land in Nutts Corner in a few minutes, only to discover that there would be no safe landing for the runways at Nutts Corner were blocked after an earlier Flying Fortress had crashed on landing.

They were unable to raise any other airfield nearby. They were losing height rapidly now so their options were few. If they delayed to jettison the equipment on board then they would probably be too low for a safe bail-out so the order was given to leave everything and bail-out. The crew bailed out at approximately 4,000 feet. The pilot and co-pilot stayed on in the hope of attempting a belly-landing but within minutes the No. 3 engine died altogether. They had no choice then but to put the aircraft on the automatic pilot and bailed out also. All members of the crew landed safely in Northern Ireland.

But the Flying Fortress was far from finished. It lumbered on, battered by a strong north-west wind. It soon drifted southwards, over the neutral Republic and its rumbling flight took it as far south as county Tipperary. The Gardaí in Roscrea heard it pass by, now apparently heading in an easterly direction. Later it appears to have circled and went southerly towards Templemore Military Barracks in County Tipperary. At 14.20 hours there it was reported by the military on duty that it was moving eastwards.

Well, now we come back to Thomas Henderson strolling across the fields of the family farm, in Johnstown, and the time about ten minutes later when the Flying Fortress decided to set herself down.

The military guard securing the area of the crash were eventually relieved by an Air Corps salvage party on the following day. They had come down from Baldonnel Aerodrome to dismantle and remove the wreckage. The salvage party, an officer and twelve men were billeted in nearby farmhouses and took fourteen days to complete their work.

Thirteen 0.50-inch machine guns, one automatic gun sight and one radio set were removed and returned to Northern Ireland. Other items salvaged included clothing, leather helmets, goggles, revolvers and ammunition along with documents and other personal items.

The Gardaí carried out house-to-house searches for items removed from the aircraft and the crash site. By all accounts they recovered many protective covers for the aircraft's gun turrets, leather flying caps with earphones, sheepskin flying trousers, gloves and boots, sleeping bags, shorts, singlets, towels, radio equipment and oxygen masks. What would anyone be doing with oxygen masks, you would wonder, way back then? But, despite all the searches, it seems that certain members of the public were seen wearing US army style pants, tunics, boots and other clothing many years after the crash.

Another story circulating around that time was that the aircraft also carried a particular alcoholic beverage, which was enjoyed by the officers. This apparently was never located either, and the reason given is that every house in the surrounding area was searched except one, and the occupier of that particular dwelling was above suspicion. But many a sing-song was facilitated thanks to the dropping in to Johnstown of the Flying Fortress on 23 January 1944.

Note: A much more detailed account of this event and others is written in the book 'Emergency' Air Incidents South-East Ireland 1940–1945 *by Patrick J. Cummins.*

6

TEARLAITH DÁ SÚILE IS A MÁTHAIR CÉILE

Mother-in-laws are a special breed of women. Some are wonderful and mind their own business but every now and then, as in all walks of life, a contrary, interfering old biddy can come along. Every county in Ireland has its share of them and Kilkenny was not over-looked in this either.

There was a man once and Tearlaith (Charles) was his name. He was, I am told, born not far from where I grew up, in south Kilkenny. This poor man, God save us all, had one eye in the front of his head and the other in the back. Now, at that time people were kinder and the only remark that was ever made was, 'Well, if God sees fit to give Tearlaith this gift of seeing what is coming and going, who are we to argue with Him?'

The people long ago really believed in God, you see, and were quite content when He made them different from each other. Sure, wasn't variety the spice of life? So Tearlaith grew up a fine strapping lad and all was well – until he fell in love with a grand girl from a neighbouring farm.

Now, that particular family had never been blessed with a son and the only daughter they had was Margaret, a lovely girl by all accounts. Well, the father died young enough, God help us, and that left Margaret and her mother to look after the farm and things became very urgent, so finally the mother agreed to the wedding.

Now, she was not what you would call a good woman for she had a bitter tongue in her head and the devil a wan went by but she had a comment of some kind or another to make on them. They were too long, too short, too stuck up, too tattered, too black, too brown, and so on and God save them if they had a mark or a blemish or the halt step for she would have words about that too. In fact, this woman could not be pleased if you stood on your head for her. She thought everyone should be as she said and should do as she bid, poor foolish soul.

Well, the wedding took place and Tearlaith moved in with Margaret into their grand new house down the lane from the old farmhouse. Sure, they weren't in there a wet day when they were joined, all uninvited, by the bitter old woman.

She knew they could never manage without her, she said, and took her belongings into the best bedroom. My own thought would be that the old rip was lonely but wouldn't admit it.

Now, she was no sooner inside on the floor than she started. He must wear a cap to cover that second eye in the back of his head.

She didn't like it that he would see when she made the 'pus' at him behind Margaret's back.

Actually she didn't like him in about the place at all and was not slow in telling him so, but he was necessary to run the farm and Margaret generally managed to keep the peace.

Then one day when she had been particularly tiresome she said to Margaret that she should be careful not to have a baby in case he would have, maybe, God save us, three eyes. Well, the poor girl, who was expecting, unknown to her mother, burst into tears and ran out to the fields to Tearlaith.

When Tearlaith saw her coming he dropped the scythe, where he was cutting the headland, and ran to her. She was distraught and eventually, when she stopped crying, they came to a decision. The mother-in-law would have to go or there would be a murder. So they went down to the parish priest and told him things were very bad and if the mother-in-law didn't move out and go back to her own place they would not be responsible for what might happen.

Well, the parish priest had only that very minute got word that his housekeeper had taken a bad tumble and broken a wrist – God works in mysterious ways. So, being anxious to help the young couple and to avoid a possible murder, he said, 'Well maybe she could move in here as my housekeeper for a while.' It was he who went up to the house to ask her, for the other two wouldn't, they were so annoyed with the old woman, and between the jigs and the reels wasn't she gone down to the parish priest's house, bag and baggage, when they did finally gather the courage to come home.

Not a note did she leave, thinking they would worry and not know where she was. But sure, they were delighted to have the kitchen to themselves, at last, and so glad were they of the peace and quiet that they just sat and ate their meal with not a word passing between them, only the odd smile. You know the way of things I am sure it has happened to yourself sometime. Peace, perfect peace.

You would think that would have been the fixing of things but only two weeks later, just as they sat to table, who did they see come skirting in the yard? Only the parish priest and sparks flying from his heels. Well, he came in and sat to the table with them and in a rush of words, not as circumspect as usual at all, he said they would have to find another cure for the mother-in-law.

She was driving him daft with her constant instructions and suggestions. Didn't she know the seed and breed of everyone who walked the parish? He couldn't look at his congregation from the pulpit without remembering the remarks the old woman passed about them all and the reams of advice on what he should do about them.

'I will end up committing the seven deadly sins, no bother,' said he, 'if we don't get her out of my house, and she's dug herself in good and proper, so she has. The sermons I give are the latest trouble. She is sure she could do them better if I would let her, God bless me and save me.'

They talked long and hard and then finally agreed. Even though the parish priest knew he should not be agreeing, they agreed to bring her to the Fairy Doctor over near Ballykeoghan. Fairy Doctors were easily found at that time and good they were at jobs the Church had no handle on. The Church was still new enough to Ireland then.

They told the old woman that the Fairy Doctor needed her advice – that was the only way she would leave the parish priest's house, for she was a great woman for giving advice, regardless of her background knowledge. Well, in they bowled to the Fairy Doctor's house and left her there. Sure, they were only gone a half an hour when the poor man had enough of her.

'This will take a little bit of something extra,' says he, throwing some herbs onto the fire. In a minute the place filled up with a grey cloudy smoke and the old woman was so busy giving out about the parish priest and everybody else that she didn't notice until she suddenly found herself out in the middle of the desert and the sun blazing down on her.

'God save us, where am I?' says she. The Fairy Doctor looked at her with his severe eye. 'You are on the road to heaven or hell, take your choice,' said he. He pointed down the road and there, by the side of the track through the sand, were hundreds and hundreds of little houses and at the door of each one stood a woman or a man and they sweeping like fury to keep out the sand that kept blowing in around the floor.

'Why are they doing that? Sure, is it daft they all are?' she asked, crossly.

'There you go again,' said the Fairy Doctor. 'Can't you be satisfied with anything the good God made? These were the very same as you. Nothing on God's earth pleased them so God decided that if they thought they could do things better than He could they might as well start by tidying up the grains of sand in the desert and see how they could make it better than he had.' She opened her mouth to say a whole fist of words but the woman nearest her gave a furious sweep of sand and she took a fit of coughing instead.

'Come on,' said the Fairy Doctor, 'I'll show you another bit' and up the track they went between clouds of sand and there in the dust she could see a great big sprawling shack of a place and people going out and in and in and out without stop. 'What is it? Who are they?'

The Fairy Doctor pointed to the sign over the door which read Last Chance Saloon and laughed, 'Who said God hasn't a sense of humour, can't you see? They are on their last chance. They gave advice to everyone about how they should come and go, regardless of what hurt they might cause you know the way – "Now if I were you I'd soon do this or that or say the other" – so now every time they come out and feel a bit of free advice coming on they have to go back inside again and reason it through.'

'The Lord save me,' says the old woman.

'Sure, He is trying his best Mam' says the Fairy Doctor.

'Take me home,' says she. 'I'm not a bit like them, so I'm not.'

The Fairy Doctor fixed her with his eye and shook his head.

'It's all right for you,' says she. 'You don't understand how a woman feels about these things. I just wanted to make things right.'

'Perhaps if I showed you some more you would feel different,' and he lifted his hand but she grabbed his arm and shook her head.

'Is it nightmares you'd be giving me, man dear? I still have time to change, haven't I?'

He nodded and in a blink she was back in the Fairy Doctor's house.

Well, it took a shake out of her let me tell you. In a while she took her belongings back up to her own house and considered herself.

Then she walked slowly down the lane and came back in on the kitchen floor where her daughter and Tearlaith were sitting at the table to their dinner.

'I'll not be staying long and will only come when you would like me to call.' Margaret got up and took down another cup and plate and set them on the table. Tearlaith never stirred but the eye at the back of his head studied the old woman carefully. She swallowed and stiffened her back, 'What I said child, I wish it unsaid for I never meant a word of it'.

Margaret looked at Tearlaith as he scraped back the chair and stood tall above the old woman. 'God help you if you ever hurt my wife or any who belong to me again.' He brushed past her and lifted the kettle from the hook above the fire to make a fresh pot of tea.

Margaret smiled at her husband. Her mother looked from one to the other – 'I was only trying to …,' says she, then she stopped and, as quick as a wink, she grabbed the sweeping brush and began to brush furiously out the back step.

Later on she had her tea and from then on they had peace and comfort, except that every so often, for no apparent reason, the old woman would go out the door then come back in real quick and make a grab for the sweeping brush and begin sweeping like mad. Only the Fairy Doctor knew why and now we know it too.

7

KILASPY HOUSE AND THE BLACK LADY'S WALK

Kilaspy (*Cill Easboig*) is situated in the parish of Slieverue in south Kilkenny. Once it was attached to the parish of Dunkitt but in 1862 the townland of Kilaspy and Ballinamona were transferred over.

The fall of Kilaspy House was literal. It crumbled and lost its togetherness over many years. It was one of the Big Houses in times gone by and housed, at one time, British soldiers who were preparing to go to war in the Crimea.

At the time of the Crimean War (1850s), Kilaspy House was owned by a man called Alexander Backas, who had inherited it from his father Robert. The house seems to have been a hub of high living, at that time, and the extensive gardens were home to many unusual trees, brought back from abroad. One particular tree in the nearby woodlands was, at that time, known as 'the parlour tree' and in later years came to be called 'the breakfast tree'.

It was a huge, ancient tree with its lower branches spreading out wide, which made it easily accessible. The remains of this tree still existed when we were children in the 1950s. It seemed to us to have been a beech tree, and even then one of the lowest branches was so big that a man could not encompass it with both arms at full stretch. We were told that in the time when Thomas Sherlock owned Kilaspy estate the custom of having meals served outdoors on the table-like branches of 'the parlour tree' started. They must have had some 'pet' days for by all accounts the weather around that time was as unpredictable as always.

When Thomas Sherlock took possession of Kilaspy he must have been well placed in the community. His love of the good life and sporting activities are reported to have been the cause of his downfall. At a time when the whole of Ireland was being ravaged by the Yeomen and the French were trying to land, the story is told that Thomas had a racehorse named Bucky Bravo and he backed his own horse to win, laying out a fortune in his certainty that the horse was unbeatable. However, there were many other forces at work and the race was fixed and when Bucko Bravo lost so too did Thomas. He lost possession of Kilaspy House as a result of his foolishness.

The house was a base for the English gentry and when the soldiers were stationed there in the mid-1800s they occupied the upper story of the house and trained daily in the grounds. When we were children my brother and the boy cousins were allowed to go up to the top storey but the girls were not permitted. My brother, God be good to him, told us afterwards that it was as well we didn't go up for it was laid out in cubicles where the soldiers lived, and on the timbers surrounding the cubicles many drawings and words had been inscribed which were not fit for any girl's eyes.

Another story which comes from that time is that of 'The Black Lady's Walk'. We were told that during the Crimean War a young lady of the house became enamoured of one of the British officers and he returned her affections. However, he was only there for a time of training while waiting for the ship which would take him and his men out of the port of Waterford and off to war against the Tsar of Russia.

It was labelled as a 'holy war' because it resulted from the killing of some Orthodox monks in Jerusalem by Roman Catholic Monks. The Tsar of Russia took the opportunity to declare war on the offenders but it was, apparently, a political stroke to take over territories which didn't belong to him.

From the English point of view it was necessary to repel the Russians in case they interfered with the trade routes they had established with India.

Whatever the young officer thought about the war he didn't want to leave his lovely young lady for very long and promised faithfully that he would be back home to Kilaspy, to claim her as his bride, in no time at all.

With great reluctance they parted and she took to wearing all black while he was gone. The poor girl, sure if she had known how long she would be wearing the black she might have given herself a few years in another colour. Well, time passed, as they say, and eventually it became evident that her lover would never return to wed her. The story tells how she pined and, as my mother's people used to say, 'she went into a decline, alanna' and eventually died.

But the story didn't end there, for shortly after she was laid gently to rest, with violets growing over her, people began to see her walking, where she had always walked, along the garden walk which went all around the estate, passing by the 'parlour tree' and through the beautiful woodland. This walk was famous because along its route, at different places, three lovely stone bridges were erected to ensure the easy continuance of the pathway. These little bridges arched high over gateways where cattle and farm carts trundled through, so no one would have to walk through mucky terrain as they trod their way in their billowing crinolines, dainty bonnets and high-buttoned boots.

Many moonlit evenings she had stood on the little bridge near the house, viewing the rising moon through the young cedar tree, listening to whispered words of love as she nestled in the arms of her lover. Her ghost is still reported as frequenting that path although the land has now been turned to agricultural use.

The house itself saw many turbulent times as the years went by but it was self-sufficient in lots of ways and had its own butchery in the basement area. A grand courtyard housed many fancy coaches and traps and had dovecotes overhead running the length of the yard. The main entrance was from the Ballyrobin road which took you up a long winding avenue to the front of the great house, with a shorter entrance from the side where the extensive walled orchards were tended, in its heyday, by many gardeners.

On the front lawn there was a beautiful tall tree, of foreign origin; the name was unknown to us but maybe my grandparents knew. We were always told how the English had hung one of their own from that tree for some treason, real or imagined.

Kilaspy House, probably because of its close proximity to the boundary between county Kilkenny and Waterford, changed hands many times with well-known Waterford names holding it. The Grubbs, the Stephens, James Cahill of Hearne and Cahills and a Miss King held possession before it came, in 1901, to the Evans family. My great-grandfather Samuel Evans and his wife Frances came there from Pontypridd, near Tonapandy in Wales and lived there with their children, Ernest, Edgar, Rena and Douglas.

We often went to Kilaspy, to visit our grandparents and great-grandparent, Granny Thomas, who always dressed in the old Welsh national costume.

I remember that the house was in a bad state of repair for a long while. My grandfather never had the same interest or enthusiasm to maintain it as his father had before him. When we went to visit, the front door had difficulty closing, as the house was starting to lean a bit. It was filled with the most wonderful artefacts and furniture.

The music room held three pianos. The grand piano was often used as a place for Grandfather to pile his dismantled clocks. He had a passion for dismantling clocks and would take them from anyone with a vague promise of fixing them.

He walked regularly to Waterford City. He was 'about his own business Missus' he used to say to Grandmother. He once reported to his wide-eyed children that the only food he got in town was soup made from children's toenails. We guess now that it was French onion soup.

There were other stories told in that grand old mansion of haunting by folk in party mood and the sounds of music and revelry echoing in the quiet of the night.

A dog, a great big hound, once owned by my uncle was often put down in the basement at night and one morning when they opened the door to let him out he ran howling out the front door and across the fields until he dashed his head against a stone wall and killed himself.

There were rumours at that time that he had accidentally found the ancient tunnel which connected the old church of Kilaspy (*Cill an Easboig*) which was sited across the road from the big house, and whatever stirred within the ancient way had driven him mad. No one dared to investigate that too closely.

When Birds Eye Frozen Foods started up and got the farmers to grow peas for them I remember Da Evans (Ernest) let out the 12-acre field so it could be set with a crop of peas. People came from everywhere just to see it.

Well, to get back to the story of the fall of Kilaspy House. There was a big storm in 1957 and Mam was concerned about the state of Kilaspy House. She had been up to the house earlier that day but had failed to persuade them to leave. That night, with the storm still raging, our Mam must have had a precognition (I think she often did about lots of things). She put on her coat and headscarf and said, 'Paddy, I don't care, I'm going up to get them out' and set off up the road again, in the wind and rain.

After a long while she came back to the door with her father, Da Evans, Sammy, her only brother, and her sister, Angela Cleary and her family. They were all in a state of shock. They had taken just a few possessions with them when they had left the house, as they were sure they would be back home when the storm was over next day. However, to their horror, as they were coming down by O'Brien's farmhouse, just below Kilaspy Cross, they heard the house fall behind them.

We all made do with beds on the floor that night and when the dawn broke the boys of the Walshe family, who farmed across from Kilaspy, came, pounding on the door to know if they were safe or lost in the rubble.

The *Munster Express* reported on the fall saying that an open book had been found on top of the rubble and the name of the book was *Weather Wisdom*.

For a long while, even after it fell down, we kept up an old tradition in our family. On nights when the moon was large in the sky we would all walk up the road from Cloone Village, just to see the moon shining through the branches of a huge cedar tree in the grounds of Kilaspy. Our pleasures were simple and our chat wonderful and there was always the possibility we might catch a glimpse of the Black Lady.

A preservation order was placed on the courtyard, the only place to remain untouched when the house fell. The once grand and busy butchery, with its beautiful arched ceilings, was buried underneath many tons of rubble. A penny-farthing bicycle stood against the courtyard wall for a long while after, and the stables and coach houses began to crumble as ivy and Mother Nature encroached.

All that remains now of a once great estate are traces of where the 'Black Lady's Walk' ran through the woods. The walled-in orchard is still there but it now houses two bungalows.

8

THE JONESES OF MULLINABRO

Mullinabro is an old estate situated on the Kilkenny side of the River Suir in the parish of Kilmacow.

When we were children, on the Cloone Road, we heard lots of stories about the Jones family who lived in Mullinabro.

Some of these were definitely told with the sole purpose of scaring the life out of us but others seem to have had some basis in fact. At the Mullinabro end of the Cloone Road there is a T-junction which was always known as Shea's Cross.

At that time there was a very big, old oak tree standing on the boundary of Jones's land, right at Shea's Cross. The favourite local story was attached to the old oak tree itself. The big, strong branches reached out across the road and it was said that it was used by two different highwaymen. A man could leap down from the large branches over the road, on top of carriages carrying the local aristocracy to functions in the various Big Houses and then it was easy to relieve them of their gold and jewellery. Once the man was on top of the carriage the other gang members would come thundering along to assist with the robbery.

One of these was said to be Crotty, the highwayman from County Waterford, who apparently covered vast distances before his betrayal by his friend Norris over in the Comeragh Mountains. It has always been a matter of debate as to how Crotty crossed the River Suir, as he was a wanted and hunted man, but that he was in Mullinabro is never disputed.

The second highwayman reputed to have used this tree for the odd dastardly robbery is Freyne the Robber. Perhaps he too was drawn to this area by the fame of the Jones' and the busy traffic between the Big Houses. It is well known that he frequented the area around Tory Hill which is not too far distant.

The locals were in the habit of gathering under the shelter of this tree in the evening for talk and fun. A game of pitch and toss or perhaps skittles would be played and many a lad tried out his first cigarette, which was more than likely a Woodbine. Sometimes they had music. That always depended on who was present. It was a time when young men would sing or whistle at the drop of a hat and many carried a mouth-organ in their pockets as easy as lads carry mobile phones in the present time.

Sheada Haberlin, light of heaven to him, would occasionally come along with his accordion and then there would be singing and dancing as well. You could dance on the road then because there was no passing traffic, except for the odd bicycle and later on O'Neill's car, which you would hear in plenty of time to clear the way.

When all was finished at the end of the evening and the moon high in the sky it was then the ghost stories would be remembered or invented. Who knows for sure anymore?

One story was about how the Joneses were not kindly disposed to anyone crossing their land or indeed raiding their orchard. The crossing of the land was an old local tradition. You went on to Joneses' land at Shea's Cross and then headed straight on until you got to the main road which went from Newrath to the bridge of Waterford.

Well, by all accounts, a member of the Jones household came out one evening with a shotgun and opened fire, missed the people but killed several crows, who were flying home to roost in the woods. One of the group, seeing the crows fall down dead, put a curse on Jones and his family and said that the day the last crow left Mullinabro so too would the Jones family.

Whether this story is true or not, I cannot tell, but this much I do know: the Jones' are long gone from Mullinabro and the lands which were crossed once, either with or without the permission, are now orchards owned by the Vogelaar family. You could just as easily see a light aircraft rise now from Jones's land as see a flock of birds, for the lady of the house, Anika Vogelaar, often touched down there when she first got her pilot's licence.

The lands in Mullinabro lay desolate for many years and Purcell kept cattle on it before it came into possession of the Vogelaars. There is a story told about this land when Cromwell was rampaging in Ireland. High in his power, he decided that one of his friends should take over the estate when he drove the resident, inserted there during Strongbow's time, from it. Apparently he didn't think much of uppity knights who believed they could run estates. It is said that he instructed a local man named Jones to meet and take his man to the estate where he would surely be employed as a reward.

The friend of Cromwell arrived long after Cromwell had passed by and, true to his word, the man named Jones met him and escorted him to Mullinabro. I do not know what station this man held in his own country but he was not impressed by Mullinabro and felt insulted that Cromwell should call him over from England to such a run-down place. By way of rebuff to Cromwell, he gave the estate to the man named Jones and returned to England. Jones was delighted with his good fortune for Mullinabro was a fine estate with good land and could be made into an even better place with a little work.

When local folklore was being collected for the Schools' Scheme 1937-39 by the Irish Folklore Commission the following story about the Jones estate turned up in the tales from St Senan's National School in the parish of Kilmacow. Kathleen Laffan, local historian, gives this account in her book *A History of Kilmacow – A South Kilkenny Parish*.

'Long ago when the Jones's were very popular in this part of the country the people used to pass through their place to Mass. Now old Jones was a black Protestant but they had a rule that if a person passed through a field for a few years without being stopped, they had a right of way of that path.

Jones knew this but he advertised for a wicked bull which he put in the field through which the people passed. This stopped them for a time. At that time bull-fighters were common and after a time one of these bull-fighters came to work with a farmer in Kilmacow. When he heard of the bull he told the farmer, who was a devout Catholic, that he would remove the obstacle if he would let him off an hour early the next Saturday evening. The farmer

agreed. When Saturday evening arrived he went and cut a half-dozen ash sapling and started off with two or three others. He got into the field without being seen by the bull. He fixed the sticks in the ground except one stick he kept in his hand. Then he let out a roar and stood behind the sticks awaiting the onslaught. The bull seeing the man rushed at him furiously. He dashed at the sticks which stuck in him. In an instant the man was on his back flogging him as hard as he could.

After a while the bull was fatigued and fell down huddled up in a heap. When the bull-fighter had rested he tied on the bull's horns a piece of paper with the words 'Be Cautious'. After that the people passed through the field to Mass.

James Walsh, Dangan, Kilmacow. Told to me by Patrick Walsh, Dangan, Railwayman, aged 50 years (26-9-'39).' 49. NFCS: 843 pg 78 50. NFCS: 843 pg 79.

When the Jones family were at the height of their power there were many comings and goings between the Big Houses in the area and close contact was always kept between Kilaspy House and the Jones of Mullinabro. There was always a story about how these two houses were connected by an underground tunnel. My grandfather lived in Kilaspy House a long time ago and this story was often mentioned but we were never allowed to search for any sign of a tunnel.

The possibility of such tunnels existing is not beyond belief for the Jones family were of an engineering frame of mind and did wonderful work in the surrounding countryside with drainage channels and *tocairs* (crossing places over a wet area) which were meant to last a long time and indeed still do today.

The need for these escape tunnels from the main houses was easy to understand in the turbulent history of the country but as to whether they stretched between the houses mentioned or came out at a safe distance has never been disclosed.

The following piece was given to me by Kees Vogelaar who moved into Mullinabro with Anneke in 1963. There was no suitable accommodation on the land at this time and they were building their own new home. Anneke, who was teaching at home in Holland, until they got established in Mullinabro knew she had to take the final step and settle in Ireland. Kees tells us:

She confiscated her parents' seaside caravan and shipped it over. We lived in that, very happy and not so comfortable for a while. One Sunday morning we woke up and we were surrounded by half a dozen other caravans and horses. The caravans were the nicely painted horse-drawn ones, much nicer than ours.

Some of the stories were told to us by two elderly Jones sisters, who visited us in the Sixties. They were the last Joneses who lived in the old house, and they remembered going to town shopping by horse and carriage.

The Joneses had a flourishing business, quarrying limestone where the Cusacks live now and transporting through Jones' wood by means of a narrow-gauge railway to the yard in Mullinabro, where it was cut, put on barges in the stream, then to Waterford on the River Suir, and from there out on to bigger vessels to Liverpool. Unfortunately the remains of the railway line were also destroyed.

The Jones family had one son and two daughters. One day the son went on horseback to Waterford to sample the pleasures of the town. Returning late, he decided to jump the gate so as not to disturb the lodge keeper at such a late hour. Unfortunately he misjudged the height of the gate and got himself impaled and died.

His sister who was very fond of him, ordered the gate lodge to be demolished and the gate closed with lock and chain, and cursed was to be anyone who opened this gate. Her ghost would waft through Jones wood long after.

In the Seventies I had a young lad working for me named Billy Fell. Billy had the job of bringing in the full apple bins. When the pickers gathered in the yard after the day's work, dusk was settling in, and Billy being a bit late to bring in the last bins, came with his tractor at neck-breaking speed without any bins and his face white as a sheet. 'What's wrong Billy?' the pickers asked him.

'I heard her, I heard her,' he shouted. Billy never returned to work.

More recently, when Spanish contractors went through the middle of Mullinabro to construct the bypass they unnecessarily destroyed Jones Wood. One of the Spanish operators wanted to go through the above mentioned gate which was still padlocked, although a bit rusty. I happened to be around and he asked me could he go through the gate to make a short cut.

My Spanish was as bad as his English, and I answered, 'No, banshees here in the wood.'

'What is banshee?' he asked.

'Banshees are bad girls,' I replied.

'We no have banshees in Spain, only good girls,' he said.

'Lucky you,' I replied, 'but do not go through this gate.'

A week later the gate was flattened and a month later the Spanish company was bankrupt.

After the gate was flattened and the wood destroyed local residents reported the wailing of a banshee in the night. It was such a frightening phenomenon that, according to the local newspaper the *Munster Express*, golfers on nearby Waterford Golf Links were reluctant to be out on the course in the late evening. Many tried to dismiss the wailing as being that of a vixen but country people know the difference and the wail of a banshee is not to be scoffed at.

Mullinabro will always be associated with the name Jones, no matter who comes or goes there. It is recorded officially that there once was a working mill located on the land and that is where the name comes from (Mullin an bro).

It is also recorded that John Hawtrey Jones lived in this place in the seventeenth century and was married to Annie Milward of Waterford.

I have found a reference to a family called Denn who once occupied the Mullinabro estate but they were apparently ousted by Cromwell and moved further north into Kilkenny.

9

THE STORY OF DAME ALICE KYTELER

This story of witchcraft and Inquisition was often told to us when we were young and I never really liked it. It was frightening on so many levels and the power of the Inquisition horrified me.

However, I recently visited Ms Nicky Flynn, the present owner of the famous Kytlers Inn, which is situated in the fantastic medieval city of Kilkenny, and found myself caught up in the strange world of the late 1200s. Sitting down to a meal under the ancient stone arches of the inn can certainly bring the story to the forefront of your mind.

Alice de Kyteler was born in Kyteler's House, Kilkenny, to wealthy Norman parents. The date of her birth is given as the year 1280, but who knows now. She would have been brought into this world with the aid of a 'goodwife' or midwife and would have more than likely been taken care of in her infant state by a wetnurse.

Life in a well-to-do Norman household would have included education for the girls as well as the boys. The boys were usually fostered off to other families, of similar standing, for their education. The education of the girls was less formal but would have included codes of conduct, where you stood in the pecking order of the aristocracy, the running of a large house and the finer and genteel occupations of ladies.

I am sure that Alice was well versed in all these skills and indeed seems to have improved on them and added a few of her own particular ideas as well.

She must have been a clever young girl for she made a good marriage to one William Outlawe, who was a banker. He was definitely a good catch, as they say, but whether Alice loved him or not who knows. He must have been quite a few years her senior to be an established banker and she was just a young girl.

However, they had a son and he too was called William. Giving birth to a son was a great boost to Alice and she was probably showered with affection and gifts from her husband. Here was a son who could follow his father's footsteps into banking. You may laugh now but that was how the gentry made their plans at that time. A male heir was all important.

It is likely also that her husband was anxious to have another son, just to be on the safe side. Children in those times sometimes died young as they had none of the medicines which we have today, poor creatures.

Well, things seem to have gone well with them for a few years but then William senior took ill and died rather suddenly. Alice and her little boy were suddenly on their own, but they were not left destitute by any means. Alice was left a wealthy widow and was still a young and attractive woman. It was no surprise therefore to people when Adam de Blund of Cullen began to pay court to Alice.

Wasn't he a great man to take on another man's son? That was the word going around. The courtship didn't last very long and soon Alice became the wife of Adam de Blund. I forgot to mention that he was a wealthy man also, so he was not, in any way, after her money.

I am afraid that Adam was not long married to Dame Alice when he too found himself dying of some strange ailment. I wonder did he wonder, or indeed did he know, that he had been given a speedy ticket to the next life? However it was, he didn't get any time to change his will, and once again Alice became a wealthy widow.

All this time young William, son of the banker, was growing and was well provided for by his doting mother.

People were beginning to look at Dame Alice with a jaundiced eye. To lose one husband could happen to anyone but to lose two, in such a short time and so suddenly in each case, seemed downright careless – if not suspicious.

Alice was wealthy now beyond all expectations and ran her hostelry business in Kyteler's Inn with skill. It was an eating house with a good reputation and ideally situated to facilitate visitors to Kilkenny City who needed a place to stay with good food as an added bonus. The local inhabitants enjoyed the warmth and welcome at the inn and many of the local gentry indulged themselves in the excellent food and wine provided by Dame Alice.

The part which was beginning to upset her neighbours was that she was managing this herself, without the aid of a strong man. No matter how wealthy a woman became, she was always a target for the men who thought she was getting above herself. The woman should, after all, know her place. Only men were capable of controlling such finance as she possessed.

Now, whether the deaths of her first two husbands were as a result of something they ate or heart attacks induced by some other means, who knows.

Alice must have known very well that she was in a dangerous situation but thought she could weather the storm. One way of doing this would have been to take on another suitable husband and keep him alive long enough for people to forget their suspicions and for their begrudgery to subside.

Not every man would rush into marriage with a woman, no matter how wealthy, who had lost two husbands in mysterious circumstances. But a man called Richard de Valle seems to have had no hesitation for he was next to find comfort in the arms of Alice Kyteler.

It is possible that he loved her and trusted that no harm would come to him. The poor man should have stayed at home with his own mother for he soon succumbed to the same mysterious illness.

I have wondered lately about the son of the banker, William. Was it he who was getting rid of the husbands? Did he see them as possible fathers of rival children for his mother's affection or his inheritance? It is said that he was of a graspying, greedy nature, though how this is known I am not sure. I find it hard to believe that Dame Alice would be that stupid. Why would she draw more trouble on herself now with a third husband?

I am sure there were many harsh words spoken about Dame Alice following the demise of her third husband but no one had any proof of wrongdoing. Alice was now wealthier than ever and business was booming.

Her son William was now running his own business where he had charge of the nearby parklands. Dame Alice organised things so that the sweepings of rubbish and waste were cleared from the city streets by night and delivered to her son for use as manure on the land. There were no street cleaners in those days and many things were discarded in the walkways and lanes of the medieval city. She was either a very clever lady who was centuries ahead of her time in doing this recycling or perhaps there was more here than meets the eye.

All would probably have passed along peacefully if Alice had not agreed to a fourth marriage. I know, it is really hard to believe.

Minny, a friend of my sister Kit, had a saying: 'Once through the hoop should be enough for any woman.' Maybe Alice never knew that. Maybe she just wanted a man in her life. That happens, they tell me.

Perhaps Alice was one of those women who had a naturally magnetic personality or was it that the men in her life wished to dominate this outrageously wealthy female. They surely can't all have fallen madly in love with her, one after the other, knowing that their predecessors had come to sudden untimely ends.

Well, for one last fling, Alice married Sir John de Poer. I hope they had a good honeymoon period because in a very short while Sir John began to feel unwell. Alice must have nursed him and taken such loving care of him that in no time at all he changed his will in favour of Alice and her son William.

It is reported that the illness took the form of his hair and nails falling out and he became sickly. I have tried to find what might cause this and there are many things but it is hard to believe that any of them could have caused the death of all the four husbands.

Mercury was one of the things which could cause such symptoms but where would Alice have access to mercury? Did she know an Alchemist or was she dabbling in things which were dangerous on other levels? Would William have had access to these sources either?

When Sir John passed away all hell broke loose. Some of his own family members were outraged and were less than circumspect in the charges they began to level against Dame Alice.

At that time, one of the worst possible charges you could bring against anyone was that of witchcraft. The relatives of Sir John were looking for the greatest possible punishment to befall Alice. They approached the then Bishop of Ossory, Richard de Lederer, who was a Franciscan from England, with their charges and demanded that he do something about this woman.

England at that time was full of witch hunters and the Church was on a roll, burning and drowning many women accused of witchcraft. If you survived the ducking in water you were a witch but if you drowned you were innocent. Who would be a witch?

Bishop de Lederer was open to their suggestions that Dame Alice had somehow bewitched Sir John to get him to change his will in her favour and the charges of witchcraft and sorcery were formally brought against her.

The bishop seems to have found the savagery associated with the Inquisition to his liking and straight away assembled a Court of Inquisition which included five knights. I have often wondered about knights but sure they were only men, when all is said and done, and they did serve the Crown, which was also the Church at that time. Several noblemen were included and we can be sure that they were all hostile to this woman who had amassed such wealth and carelessly lost four husbands.

It was declared that Alice was the head of a coven of witches and had sex with a demon called Artisson, who is sometimes depicted as Aethiops, the mythical founder of Ethiopia.

Would anyone get away with such a claim today?

Alice was not standing by idly while all this was being done by Sir John's relatives and the bishop. She had her own people who did their best to defend and protect her and, despite the bishop's best efforts, he could not get the Temporal Authority to arrest and condemn Alice. He wanted to make a clean sweep of the den of iniquity so he went after her son William and her unfortunate friends and servants.

The bishop apparently wrote to the Chancellor of Ireland, Roger Outlawe, demanding to have Alice arrested. But he misjudged badly in doing this for Roger was Alice's brother-in-law. The bishop found himself incarcerated in Kilkenny by Sir Arnold le Poer, who was another brother-in-law of Alice's and also seneschal of Kilkenny. The poor bishop didn't know where to turn.

Even the brother of the late Sir John was against him. You would think that this would have given the bishop cause for pause, but no, he went ahead again as soon as he was released from prison.

The charges against Alice became more outrageous by the day. It was said that she had in her employ many unearthly creatures which only came out at night to sweep the filth from the streets of Kilkenny so that her son would prosper from their work.

She was said to ride upon a broomstick, accompanied by her two maids, Petronilla and Basila, to meet with other enchanters, who were, of course, nameless. But most fascinating of all the wild stories was the fact that she was said to have received a pot of special ointment from the demon to oil her broomstick. Surely even the bishop himself must have laughed at this one.

A finer tale still was that after holding nightly conferences with Robin Artisson, the evil spirit, the ladies would sacrifice nine red peacocks in the middle of the highway and offer up their eyes. The mind boggles. There was a great storyteller somewhere in the background surely.

But no, the bishop didn't laugh, indeed he seems to have delighted in all these fantastical stories and eagerly passed them on. He would have his Inquisition no matter what. No mere woman was going to get the better of him.

Alice was no fool and took herself off to England. This was curious as England would have been dangerous for her too if the bishop got his way, but she must have had a plan to lose herself in some out of the way place or in the thick of some city. Apparently she slipped away from Ireland in the company of just one of her maids.

This is where I fall out with Alice. Why didn't she take her son and all her maidservants with her?

Did she misjudge the animosity of the bishop? Did she think they would be safe once she left?

Or, and this is also a fearful possibility, if she had not been the one who did away with her many husbands, was she now fearful for her own safety? Was William the real villain? Would she be next?

Well, leave them behind she did and she herself disappeared into the unknown. The bishop must have been frothing because he now pursued those left behind. He would exact terrible vengeance on the friends and servants of Alice. The poor, unfortunate maidservant Petronella was to suffer the worst of all. She was tortured and flogged and, not satisfied with this, the bishop had her burned at the stake. Wouldn't you wonder about religion?

William, son and possible villain, got off very lightly indeed. Some say that all he had to do was to attend three masses a day and give alms to the poor. He was by this time a very wealthy man so it was no hardship for him. Some say that he re-roofed St Canice's Cathedral as part of his repentance.

Alice never showed herself in Kilkenny or indeed in Ireland ever again and all we can say is, small blame to her.

This story is also portrayed in much more detail by author Claire Nolan in her book The Stone. *Her publication is, in itself, another tale of interest involving the American artist Paddy Shaw and his portrait of Dame Alice. He painted the portrait many years before Claire wrote her book, and had never met her, yet when the two came together, the similarity of looks between his depiction of Dame Alice and author Claire were startling.*

The portrait now hangs in Kytelers Inn, with a note from Paddy Shaw which says, 'I painted this piece for myself. It doesn't like living with me. I think she wants to go home. So have her.'

10

THE COUNTESS OF ORMOND AND GRANNAGH CASTLE

Did you ever hear the story about Grannagh Castle and the Countess of Ormond and her infamous antics there? Well, let me tell you now that in its heyday Grannagh Castle was a very impressive river fortress.

They say it was built on the site of an ancient dún, as the site was perfect for keeping watch on the comings and goings on the River Suir. Both sides of the river were, at that time, under the control of the latest invaders, the Normans. The de la Poers were fond of building sturdy places, like all the newcomers. It gave them a sense of security and, of course, it was a way of saying 'I am here to stay and be hanged to ye'.

Now the de la Poers, or Powers as they came to be called, were uneasy neighbours for anyone to have, and they had a fondness for raiding the old Viking city of Waterford. It is said that they got much enjoyment from these forays, and later descendants carried on the same way up until Cromwell arrived in 1650. There was not much enjoyment for anyone after that.

Well, to get back to my story, the de la Poers misjudged the temperament of their own overlord, Edward III of England. He was not happy with their continuous raiding of Waterford City, as it was a very useful port for him and, to their great dismay, the de la Powers found themselves ousted from their grand castle on the banks of the Suir.

The king then installed his friends, at that moment, the Butlers of Ormond who gladly occupied it and made it a secure base for a long time to come. It was to this castle that the Great Countess of Ormond came eventually, and her coming brought fear and terror to the local inhabitants.

Now, how she came to be so hard-hearted is difficult to understand, so if you will allow, I will start at the beginning with her own story.

She was the daughter of Gerald Mór Fitzgerald, the 8th Earl of Kildare, and of Alison FitzEustace. Both families were steeped in duty and tradition.

Mairead ní Gerroid (Margaret Fitzgerald) was sometimes called Magheen, in the perverse humour of the Irish, for Magheen is 'little Margaret', and anyone with an eye in their head could see that she would be many things but never 'little', for she was growing like a weed, bless her.

She was twelve. A young girl, tall for her age, pretty by all accounts, and soon to be married. She was to marry a boy who was unknown to her, the son of the bitter enemies of her family.

The Butlers of Ormond were offering their son, Piers, as a husband for her. It was all for political gain, for power, something the children of the ruling classes, of the time, understood only too well.

It must have terrified her, the poor child, but she had courage flowing through her veins, the courage of 'The Geraldines'. Later, she would use 'The Geraldines' as a reminder to many that she was not to be trifled with.

It was a turbulent time in Irish history, and the blending of the old Gaelic families and the, now resident, invaders, the Normans, was not going well.

Margaret was swept into marriage with Piers Butler in an effort to facilitate kinship between the Geraldines and the Butlers of Ormond. It was also hoped that it would put an end to the long drawn-out bitterness between these two powerful families. But sure, you and I know that it is never as easy as that to make peace between people. As they say, some have long memories.

It is easy to imagine the young couple thinking that they would be taken care of yet a while, only to find that a dastardly relative, an illegitimate nephew of Thomas Butler, the 7th Earl of Ormond, who lived in England, was going to hound them out of everything if he could.

He was known as James Dubh Butler. *Dubh* means black, and he was black by name and nature the same lad. Now Margaret's husband, Piers, had a second name too, and it was *Ruadh* or red, and even though he endured the persecution from James Dubh for almost twelve years, talk about slow to anger, he finally came to blows with him and killed him in a skirmish. Some say it was an ambush but sure, we weren't there so who can tell.

Can't you see them now, riding out with some of their followers, in all their Norman finery, and coming on each other? Then the flare of anger and the shouted abuse, horses plunging forward and the clash of swords. Piers must have known great exultation when he put paid to his deadly enemy, but he would also have known that he was in grave trouble. It could well have been the end of Piers and Margaret, but his luck had turned, and he was granted a pardon in the following year.

Sure, everyone knew the blackguarding which had gone on beforehand, and Margaret's family, the Fitzgeralds, were a force to be reckoned with.

Immediately he got his pardon the bould Piers took the bull by the horns and ousted the followers of James Dubh and moved into Kilkenny Castle with Margaret. They made it their first real home. All the years of struggling for a place of their own were now a distant memory, and you can say what you like about Piers Ruadh Butler, but you can't deny he provided a most excellent home for his young wife. Margaret would have been around twenty-five years of age when she entered into Kilkenny Castle carrying her baby son James, who was only one year old.

Can you imagine how she must have felt as she stepped across the threshold? It was not as grand a castle as it was to become in the years that followed. Margaret was gifted with enthusiasm and ability. She quickly took charge, and in the next seventeen years she worked diligently, and the lives of those who lived within the castle confines and surrounding areas improved beyond recognition.

We would be foolish to think that her life was now free from worry for it was anything but. Piers had to constantly fight off enemies, and guard the borders of his domain. There were constant insurrections among the suppressed native Irish population. It was a time of great upheaval. Piers was also answerable to the English Crown and did his best to be loyal to his king.

His fortunes rose and fell. At one time he held the position of Lord Deputy of Ireland, and another time he was struggling against his in-laws, the Fitzgeralds, who joined with the dreaded O'Neills, and ravaged the county of Kilkenny. Margaret's brother Gearóid Óg became Earl of Kildare on the death of their father in 1513.

Her husband and brother were constantly being called before the king in England to sort out their differences. She must have been at her wits' end with the two of them.

When the 7th Earl died in 1515, Piers became the 8th Earl of Ormond and Margaret was now Countess of Ormond. By this stage she had given birth several times. Her first three children were boys, and this must have given them great joy, and their enemies many headaches.

Afterwards, she gave birth to six girls who made good marriages, which was something the aristocracy were good at arranging then.

Piers was ambitious in his own way, and, ably assisted by Margaret, he saw that the people who depended upon them were well cared for. They say that she planted the idea in his head that he should invite over to Kilkenny some Flemish craftsmen who set up a weaving industry.

You will recall that I said one of the reasons for their marriage, in the first instance, was to make peace between the two families. Well, unfortunately it didn't work for there was always rancour just beneath the surface, and at one stage it is reported that Piers had a serious falling out with one of Margaret's relatives, James Fitzgerald, for the unlawful killing of one of his men, James Talbot. He pursued him for this, even bringing him before the justice of the King of England. The result was that James Fitzgerald was sentenced to walk through the streets of London as a prisoner with a halter around his neck.

It would be wrong to think that Margaret sat at home in Kilkenny, twiddling her thumbs, while Piers had all the action. It can be seen from many old records that she too was over and back to London many times. She was also buying fittings and tapestries for the different castles she was building around the county such as Gowran and Ballyragget.

It was Margaret who saw to it that a school was founded. Margaret herself must have had a good education, for she is reputed to have been very clever and knowledgeable about many things. She must have continued with her education after she married Piers, for remember that she was only twelve years old at that time.

About thirteen years after he became Earl of Ormond, Piers was approached by some very powerful people who advised him to give up his title as Earl of Ormond in favour of Thomas, a grandson of the 7th Earl. Now, here is the thing you probably never knew. The grandson to whom Piers gave way was none other than Thomas Boleyn, father of Anne Boleyn. Piers had no choice. He was up against King Henry VIII, who had his eye on Anne Boleyn, and by taking the title from Piers and giving it to her father he doing the old coaxieorum on a grand scale. Well, we all know how that ended. Beware the eye of a king.

I am sure that Margaret was fit to be tied. All the work, all the building of a power base, and it to be taken away just like that, at the whim of a monarch trying to impress a young girl. It is small wonder that she was in a towering rage when she descended on Grannagh Castle.

Now, she had been instrumental in the building of other castles in the county but her choice, when she had to leave Kilkenny, was to head to the stronghold of Grannagh. It was the most important castle next to Kilkenny Castle and it took her far enough away so as not to be coming face to face with Thomas Boleyn and his people on an everyday basis.

Oh, there were compensations, to be sure, but the title 1st Earl of Ossory, for Piers, in no way compensated the Countess for her loss.

She had always been clever in legal matters and in building castles, and could see ahead where complications might arise. They say that she was the real driving force behind Piers Ormond. This is often the case, even today, that a strong woman makes the running. Margaret was the person with whom the great and good consulted when building or making decisions, or indeed any important work.

However, when she came to reside on the banks of the Suir she was out of reach and out of touch with her beloved Kilkenny Castle, and must have felt the isolation. When she had made as many alterations to Grannagh Castle as she could, she had time on her hands.

This is where the stories about Countess Margaret of Ormond take a sinister turn. It is said that she became very temperamental and dangerous to cross. I wonder now, was she in the grip of a change of life in more ways than one?

Perhaps she had inherited the strange gift which her father Gearoid Mor is said to have had, and it came to the fore at that time. According to legend he was well versed in the mystical arts and could shapeshift, as could all descendants of the ancient Tuath de Dannan race. Sure, what do any of us know about those times? If they could do those things they could have got rid of James Dubh Butler much sooner.

But one famous story tells how she demanded that the resident castle jester, in Grannagh Castle, should entertain her and raise her spirits, and the poor cratur did his best. He could see that she was not impressed no matter how hard he tried, so in a desperate effort to please her, he demonstrated how he could make several rope nooses from the one piece of rope.

The Countess was in a vicious frame of mind and on seeing this she challenged the jester saying that it would never work for a multiple hanging. You can imagine the terrified state the jester was in now. The Countess was determined to do mischief and sent her soldiers to round up several peasants and warned the poor jester that if the invention was not successful, he would hang too.

The cratur had only meant her to admire his dexterity with the rope and now here it was gone out of all control. The soldiers brought in the unfortunate people and on her command, hung the craturs from the battlements. The jester was safe for another while.

Some say that around about this time the Countess became involved with dark practices, but we have no way of knowing, and in any case who was there to challenge her. She was powerful and demanded obedience from the powerless under her control. Power is a terrible thing, especially when it is abused.

While in Grannagh, it is said that she was a regular visitor to the home of the Mandeville family. She much admired their Manor House, and demanded that they hand it over for her use. When they declined it is said that she cursed their children. It is reported that they had sixteen sons and they all subsequently died, bless us and save us.

Another tale, about how she robbed and murdered seven brothers, runs like this.

It happened one time in the county that a woman gave birth to seven sons at the one birthing, bless us and save us all. It seems they were little, as one might imagine with so many of them birthing like that, and their father, fearing witchcraft was involved, decided to drown the lot of them, like pups in a bag. This may have been an excuse, as he was desperately poor and had no means of supporting seven sons.

He was on his way to the river to carry out this terrible deed when he met a holy man, and the holy man could see straight away what his purpose was. When he challenged their father as to what was in the bag, he answered that they were just a litter of pups he couldn't care for so he was drowning them. The little boys in the sack began crying weakly and the holy man gave one look at him and reached his hand for the sack. The father did not resist, but turned away in shame and sorrow. The holy man took the seven little boys from him and away out of the area altogether, to raise them himself.

The holy man educated them so well that soon they were in Rome to be made bishops by the Pope. When they were consecrated bishops the holy man, who was now very old, made them promise to return to Ireland and to spread the Christian faith, which task he had given up in order to take care of them. The seven bishops set out for Ireland and came into the Port of Waterford.

It was normal in those times for travellers to wear hooded robes, and this is how they were dressed as they set out to complete their tasks. They had to pass by Grannagh Castle as they journeyed, and naturally enough the resident Countess of Ormond knew already that seven robed strangers were passing through her estate. It is said that she watched them pass, and seeing they each carried a pack and wore expensive-looking rings, she deduced that they were wealthy.

They had no sooner gone by the castle than she had, what my mother would have called a '*raisch*', and decided that they were concealing gold from her. She was probably right that they had gold for they may well have had a chalice of gold or gold cross for use as practicing bishops. The Countess sent her men after them with instructions to get rid of them and bring back their gold.

It is said that the seven bishops were murdered at a place known as Ath na gCeann, on the Lismatigue River in Aghavillar, in County Kilkenny.

When the Countess saw what was returned to her she realised that she had committed a grievous error, and this seemed to drive her only to further excesses.

Ten years after Piers had given up his earldom, Tom Boleyn died and Piers was restored to his title. They moved back into Kilkenny Castle. It was too late for them to get settled again and enjoy their former high status. Within a year Piers died, leaving the Countess to her own devices.

Three years later Margaret Countess of Ormond passed away, by which time she had become known as Chuntaois mhalaithe or the Cursed Countess.

They are buried side by side in St Canice's Cathedral in Kilkenny. Their effigies adorn the tomb, so if you wish to get a glimpse of a woman who was famous for both kindness and cruelty, why don't you make your way there.

11

THE
CONNAWEE

There was a quarry up in Davidstown, which was in use when I was a child. Often I would hear my father say to my mother, 'I am off up to the Connawee today.' We were a curious family and in the evening time, with the Rosary said and the kettle singing and the fire radiating its heat into the kitchen, we would ask Da about the name Connawee.

His explanation would come with many stops and starts to drink his cup of tea. He was fond of tea, our Da.

'It is a long way up a steep hill to get to it and I will take ye there one day when ye are bigger,' was his promise. Well, that delighted us straight away.

'It is an old story,' said he, 'and I am not sure I have the rights of it but we will give it a go.'

By then the only sounds in the kitchen were the ticking clock on the mantelpiece, the singing kettle, Ma's knitting needles doing a soft click clack and the sparking of logs in the fire.

'St Patrick,' said he, 'was a strange man.'

'But very holy,' interrupted my mother.

'Oh aye, very, very holy indeed. But he was a man like any other and sometimes he wandered in high and strange places. He was always looking to convert the native Irish people. He saw it as his duty before God and indeed maybe it was for he was a man who had many visions and talked with angels, they say. But then all the holy men long ago seemed to do that,' he added matter-of-factly.

We knew no different so we listened and learned.

'Did you know that St Patrick was fond of Kilkenny and wanted to have churches built up and down the length and breadth of it? Now you understand that it wasn't called Kilkenny then, but that is another story. We will stick with St Patrick and his roaming for this night.'

'Up near the Connawee he was talking with the local tribesmen and trying to convert them to Christianity. He was a brave man, I will give him that.'

'Some people were very interested in what he had to say but a lot of the people there would have been worshippers of different gods. Not bad gods now or anything like that. They worshipped the sun because it warmed them and grew their crops. They worshipped the rivers because they gave them water, and some worshipped Mother Earth herself and the trees and things like that. It was a very long time ago and there were druids instead of priests.'

'Well, when he came to this area he found his way up towards Culnaleen and turned off there for Cat's Rock. You know the Irish for that now don't ye, Carraig an Chait. Then just as he turned off, where Cullen's shop is on the fork of the road, didn't he stop for a drink at a little well and that blessed well is there to this very day and it is called St Patrick's well. Sure, we can cycle there on Sunday and I can show ye.'

He had us now; we loved to go with him on these adventures.

'When he finished his drink and rested a while, St Patrick headed off towards Davidstown, where he was to meet with the local chieftain and his people. He was already on the high ground so didn't have to climb that narrow steep hill where I go to the quarry at all. No, he was high up alright. He thought he was doing great with his conversions now and maybe he could get the locals to build a church for Christian worship. Ah the poor foolish saint, he didn't know the crowd he was dealing with at all.

'Sure, they welcomed him in and some were kind to him but they laughed behind his back, which was not right by the laws of hospitality. You know the old way was that if you shared your food, or as they used to say 'shared salt' with a person, then you were forbidden to do them any harm in your home or your land.

'When they said they would prepare a feast in his honour, St Patrick thought he and his followers were home and dry. Ah woe is me. The way I heard it as a child, was that the chieftain in the lands around Ballincrea, where they were, was a nasty piece of work and he gave orders to the women, who were doing the cooking, to cook up a greyhound and serve it up on a platter to the saint.

'They say that his reason was that if St Patrick was as holy as he was making himself out to be and a servant of the True God, then he would know enough not to eat the meat of the hound, which was poisoned for good measure.

'Well, in no time at all, the fires were blazing and the clan gathered on that high place and the saint and his followers sat down to the feast. The serving woman came and laid up the roasted hound in front of St Patrick.

'St Patrick was not foolish. He had noticed how some had sneered when he spoke of the One True God. He had sensed the falseness in the welcome he had received from the chieftain of the clan and he was suspicious. He made a sign to his followers and they all kept their hands away from the food and St Patrick stood up and thanked his host for the food provided and now says he, "I will thank the One True God and ask him to bless this food laid out here for us".

'He must have seen the looks on the faces of those who knew about the greyhound but he continued and, stretching out his hands he made the sign of the cross over the roasted meat on the platter. Maybe he asked God to return the creature to its original shape or maybe he just blessed his food and thanked God as we do today before we eat. Whatever he did, didn't the roasted meat begin to tremble and in a flash there, standing on four long legs, was a yellow hound which let out an unearthly cry and leapt from the dish and took off across the countryside.

'The chieftain knew at once that he had made a terrible mistake and fell on his knees before the saint. St Patrick said nothing to him yet a while and turned to the men who were in the company and told them to find the poor animal and kill it decently and bury it beneath the earth. Well, need I tell you that everyone there was

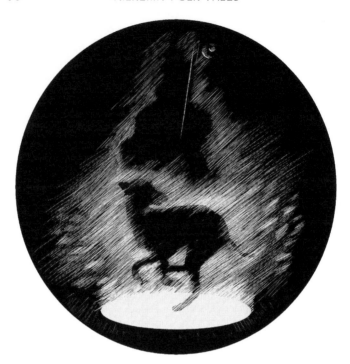

more than ready to listen to the saint after that and they took off
after the poor hound and, finding it after many the long mile, they
did as the saint instructed.

'Some say that the hound's footprints were to be found on many
rocks that it touched and indeed didn't we find one such rock
ourselves in the stream outside the house here, which flows through
Jimmy Brien's fields.'

We nodded speechless for indeed we had wondered about that
imprint of a hound's paw for a long time and here at last was a most
unexpected answer.

'While they were off chasing the poor hound, St Patrick turned
to his new converts and sure he could see into the hearts of them
and he knelt down on a big stone and the imprints of his knees
sank into the stone and he put the name Connawee on the place,
meaning yellow hound (*Cuin bhuide*) and that name is still on that
area to this very day.

'Saints then had great power and sometimes you would wonder at the things they did, but it is said, and I have no proof of this, that St Patrick put a curse on the people of that place and he walked away from it and never thought to build a church, to the One True God, there again.'

My father lifted the teacup to his lips and seemed surprised to find he had already finished the last drop. He sighed and caught my mother's eye and they both smiled.

We were always quiet after a story, mulling it around in our own ways, but I can still hear the echo of my father's voice whenever I recall the stories he told us.

The stream outside the house where my sister Kit and brother Seamus found the slab of rock with the imprint of the hound's paw now lies under the new road which cuts across the top of Cloone Hill. I don't expect those laying the road ever noticed it. Perhaps it was the print from another poor animal, long forgotten, who passed that way when the world was fresh and young.

I have heard several versions of this story and even the words of the curse which it is said St Patrick put on the people of Ballincrea, rattled off in a sing-song manner by people who obviously knew it since their childhood years.

Some part of me is reluctant to set it down here as though it would re-enforce it. However, in the interest of recording the folklore of the place, I will include just the first part of St Patrick's Curse.

> Accursed be Ballincrea's people,
> From whom the hound was sent to me
> As long as bell shall ring in steeple
> As long as man and time shall be
> Accursed the black breed of the woman
> Who served to me this filthy hound.

The curse proceeds to detail the terrible fate which is to befall the people who served the hound. I have heard it said, even recently, that people in the surrounding areas still believe this curse to be on the descendants of that tribe.

There is still another version of this story to be found in a book called *Sliabh Rua: A History of its People and Places*. In that book it is called *The Legend of the Yellow Hound (Coin Bhuidhe) Schools Collection*. It is taken from the collection by the Irish Folklore Commission and registered as IFC 845/68.

That version of the story relates how the men pursued the hound and killed her near a place called Treanaree. They buried her there and over her grave a small stunted whitethorn bush is now to be seen, called *Sgcithin na con* (meaning the little thorn of the hound). The stones near the bush are impressed with the marks of the grey-hound's feet and one of them exhibits the figure of the greyhound in miniature.

If my father knew this part of the legend, he never told us. Perhaps he didn't want us trying to find it by ourselves or more than likely he felt my mother's warning eye on him.

12

AN tSEAN BHÓ RIABHACH
(THE OLD BRINDLED COW)

*This folktale is common amongst most country folk, up and down the country,
but it was in Kilkenny I first heard it so I am including it in this collection.*

The weather had been very unsettled and was making no real effort
to be kind. The month of April should see a bit of settling after the
blustery, windy March, but here we were almost into April and still
the bitter winds persisted.

My mother was making bread in the kitchen when her friend
Hannie Maher came in with a baby on her hip. 'Bless us and save us,
isn't it terrible weather altogether and the days of the Old Brindled
Cow yet to come.' Our mother laughed and said, 'I haven't heard
that said in a long while but you are right. The children won't be
wearing little white ankle socks this Easter if this keeps up.'

We were not anxious to get into the little white ankle socks, but
Easter Sunday was the day when the ankle socks were worn each
year and then you were in them for the summer. Sure, to have ankle
socks was a great thing because it wasn't long after the war and many
the boy and girl had gone barefoot through the summer months in
the years gone by.

Later on, when Hannie was gone home to her own house, and we
were sat around the table, having our supper, we asked about the
brindle cow. My dad's head came up like someone getting the scent
of roast turkey on Christmas Eve. My mother laughed. 'Couldn't ye
have waited until we finished the bit of food?' He wanted to know

who mentioned the brindle cow and when we said it was Hannie he nodded wisely. 'Aye, Hannie would know alright.'

After that it was easy to get him to tell us what he knew. I know now that the storyteller in my father often gave him leave to shape stories in a way we could understand them better and remember them.

He started by reminding us about the 'black bog' over near Ballinamona, where our Auntie Mary and Uncle Douglas lived. Often he would point it out to us, when we cycled to the Mile Post or Slieverue. He always warned us never to go picking blackberries there, he even reminded us about it when they weren't in season, God help us. But sure, you had to listen to parents then.

We always sensed an edge of fear to his voice when he told us that, beyond the road ditch, there were unmarked bottomless bog holes. He would shake his head and tell us that many a good beast had been lost there and once, that he knew of, and here he would sign himself with the cross, a poor man was lost trying to drag out a straying donkey.

It always frightened us to think of the bottomless bog, but what had that to do with the brindled cow? This is how he told the story, once he had planted the 'black bog' in our imaginations.

The Friday coming will be the first day of April and that is the first of three days of the old brindled cow. A brindled cow is just like some of the cows you see going home, up the road, for milking. You know the ones, with the brownish stripes down their sides.

Well, when the world was young things were much different than they are now. Nature was wilder and freer and the elements and creatures of the earth could converse with each other, if they so desired.

Now, the old brindled cow was tired after the hard winter and then the constant blowing of the bitter March wind. She grumbled every day to the rest of the herd that it was the worst March she had ever known. She was just getting old, the cratur, I think. So it was small wonder then when the first hint of the soft days came, just before the beginning of April, her spirits lifted and she was, like ourselves, delighted with the bit of warm sunshine on her back. Sure, the cratur frolicked around like a young spring lamb and headed towards the greenest patches of grass she could see on the edge of the high bog.

But the old month of March was a bit fed up himself, as he listened to her grumbling, week in week out. As a matter of fact, he had a name for the Old Brindled Cow and it was 'Moan-a-lot'. Neither was he ready to give up his puffing and blowing just yet, so he approached the gentler month of April and asked if he could have just three more days to use up all his old wind.

April is a giddy month, as you well know, with her sunshine and showers, and she laughingly replied that she would give him the three days if he would marry her.

March had never considered marriage before, indeed he is so cruel and hard it is easy to see why no one had asked him to get married before this. He thought about it a minute and decided that, in order to get his three days, he would give it a try.

Unfortunately the old brindled cow did not hear them make the bargain for she was nuzzling and munching the fresh green grass and licking her lips loudly. She did not know that March was annoyed

with her complaining and moaning about him. So there she was up on the edge of the high bog when March began to blow his strongest icy winds from the east.

March is famous for his buffeting wind. He blows in great big gusts, often blowing roofs off the barns and tipping the empty milk churns over and sometimes even wrecking ships, bless us and save us. When he loses his head it is time to watch out. Most trees know when to bend with the wind but even trees can get caught out by March wind.

It was no wonder then that the poor brindled cow struggled to keep her balance as she teetered on the very brink of the bog. With one great whoosh she was swept off her feet and into the bottomless bog hole. She never came up.

April was not happy about that, and who can blame her, so she told March that she had changed her mind and didn't want to marry him after all. She had a lucky escape is all I can say. March didn't really care but he comes and claims his three days whenever the notion takes him. Those are the times when April feels like March and if it is the 1, 2 and 3 April those days are called the Days of the Old Brindled Cow.

So now you know the story of the old brindled cow and let you keep an eye on next April and see if March comes to claim his three days.

Note: This tale is told in many countries with their own twist to it. Even here in Ireland there are variations, i.e. according to that famous old Irish writer Amhlaoibh O'Súlleabháin, author of *Cín Lae Amhlaoibh*, the days called *Laethanta na Riabhaiche*, are 12, 13 and 14 April. In some parts of the West they count the last three days of March and the first three days of April.

I got this following verse from Paddy O'Connor, a travelling man:

> The first of them was wind and wet
> The second of them was snow and sleet
> The third of them was such a freeze
> It froze the birds' claws to the trees.

He told me that there were other verses but he misremembered them so we talked on about hard winters where the feet of poor beasts were frozen to the ground, but that is another tale entirely.

I give you this information in case you ever get into an argument about it. As you and I know some people can be very sure that they alone are right.

13

LOUGH CULLEN
(HOLLY LAKE)

*There are many versions of this story and some are more detailed and
have different emphases to the tale told here.*

When we moved to live on the Cloone Road in 1950 my father
was working for the Kilkenny County Council so he was often in
the quarry known as Charlestown quarry. Sometimes we would
cycle over as far as the quarry just to see where the big crusher was
working, or after they had set off dynamite, blasting the rocks.

The word would be sent out to the surrounding countryside that the
blasting would be taking place on this day or that, at this time or that,
and everyone was to stay clear of the area. The local Gardaí would be
on hand too, to make sure everything was in order and that no foolish
garsún (young boy) would be tempted to go too near the quarry.

Well, it was on one such day, when we were chatting on the road
outside the quarry gates, that my father warned us not to be going
over near Holly Lake, which was just across the fields on the far side
of the road. Sure, the poor man should never have mentioned it at
all for it was like honey to bees. Nothing would do us only try and
find out all we could about this hidden lake and pester him to know
the best way to get to it.

In our minds we saw a lovely lake with strong green, tree-covered
banks, probably holly trees as that was the name of the lake.
We couldn't have been more wrong. The lake is in the centre of a vast
spread of wetlands and bogs. No place for foolish children.

I think the poor man realised his mistake straight away, probably from the light in our eyes. To correct this he began to tell us the story of Holly Lake or Loch Cuileann, which was the old name for it and is still on some maps today.

In the long time ago when the world was a young, and people new to it, there were many forests and broad stretches of flat land as well. People had different beliefs then and one of them, by all accounts, was that people would gather on Tory Hill which stands high above the plain of Loch Cuileann, and part of their worship was to bless the sun which warmed them and helped grow their crops.

When they were finished their celebrating they would scatter first along the side of Tory Hill and gather the berries from the stunted bushes or *frachan*, as some called it. They had another name for the berries as well, they were called 'hurts', and they were like the blueberries which we buy in the shops today. These they would eat as they picked, or gather to take away home for later. Then down the hill they would proceed, until they came to the flatland around Loch Cuileann. I suppose they were like all people to this day, when they had finished worshipping they felt it was right to enjoy a bit of sport.

The sport of the time was hurling. Not the grand, elegant hurling of today with young men being sponsored and all that kind of thing, special hurleys and footgear, not at all. Even their camans (hurleys) were not the same as those used today. Theirs were made from different wood entirely. It is said that the camans they used that day were made of holly and hazel. My father would have us believe that one team had holly and the other hazel, but we thought he was stretching the story there. But, sure, what did we know? The only thing I can be sure of now is that the most popular wood today, for hurley making, is the ash.

Well, to make a long story short, they descended on the plain, now known as Lough Cullen, in great numbers and divided into two groups. No, there was no counting off of fifteen players, with a few subs as they have today. They all got involved in the great game. Great it was on the day in question, for it is said that there were as many as sixty players on either side, out there on the *faiche* (green area).

They faced up to each other with might and main and it was the game of all times on that wide plain. They ducked and dodged, bent, lifted, struck, hounded and harried until they were teeming with perspiration and high with the exultation of it all. They were like warriors engaged in a mighty battle. Every now and again a man or lad would drop out for a breather, only to be swept in again as the ebb and flow of the game came near to him.

This was how it happened that a young player of the grand game came to the sideline of the fray, and his need was more for a drink of cool water than anything else. There were many streams and trickles of water coming down from the Tory Hill side of the plain, but where this young warrior stepped out looking for a drink he could see no sign of water.

There were followers and families watching this game and he approached an old woman standing nearby. She looked as if she was from the place, so he thought she should know where he might find the nearest drinking water so he could return to the game quickly.

It is said that, in his haste, he lacked manners when he spoke to her and she was not pleased. She did, however, direct him to a clump of rushes and told him he might find water underneath, but he was to be sure to replace the plug of rushes into the hole immediately after.

Young men can sometimes be ungracious and hasty and, turning away from her, he pulled the plug of rushes and, sure enough, crystal clear water bubbled up from underneath. He slaked his thirst and, conscious all the time of the movement of the game, he was eager to re-join his companions. Whether he just forgot in the excitement, or whether he did it out of disrespect to the old woman, it is not clear, but he neglected to put back in the plug of rushes and hurried back to play.

It is said the old woman began to murmur angry words when she saw his act of foolishness and disrespect. She may even have moved towards the spot to replace the plug of rushes herself, but she was slow and old, bless her, and in a very short minute the bubbling spring began to pour out in a manner never seen before. Like an underground river unleashed, it poured and spread with unbelievable speed across the flat land of the plain.

People on the edge of the game, alerted by the cries of their friends, managed to scramble to higher ground, but the players were so engrossed in the game that they mistook the cries of alarm for cries of support and, in what seemed to many to be only a breath or two later, all the players of that grand game were swept away in the flood, and only their camans remained floating on the great expanse of water which now filled the faiche.

There was great lamenting and *olagóning* and it is said that the old woman was heard crying out distractedly '*An luachair, an luachair*'. ('The rushes, the rushes.') But it was too late as the clump of rushes was washed away with everything else.

When the waters finally settled there was this long lake in the centre of a great soggy wetland, and that is what is still there to this very day.

Some say that if there is a full moon around midsummer that the water of the lake becomes turbulent and the ghosts of the drowned young men can be seen in ghostly combat, with their camans of holly and hazel, out over the water.

We listened to our father with great wonder and more than a little shiver of fear.

'Was she a witch do you think?' we asked. 'If she was putting a curse on him why was she shouting about the rushes?'

'I don't know if she was anything more than an old woman who was tormented when he didn't do what he was told. Maybe she knew the harm that one foolish person can cause many others. Indeed, I often mutter under my breath myself these days. Let ye be away home now and not be worrying your mother.'

We did journey to a little bridge over a stream just a little way up the road from the quarry, and we viewed the dun-coloured water there which flows out from Lough Cullen onward to join the River Suir. The banks looked sturdy enough to us, but you could see that further in they began to fall away to soggy wet ground.

We never did manage to get out to Holly Lake, but fishermen have made the journey regularly, and there is a preservation order on that whole area now as some of it is unique and so the birds that frequent it are safe under the law of the land.

People still journey to Tory Hill on the second Sunday in July, which is known in the area as Pattern Sunday. You can still pick the 'hurts' on the side of the hill if you are of a mind so to do, and Lough Cullen is clearly visible with its floodplain stretching out into the local farmers' fields.

On the top of Tory Hill today there stands a Marian Year Cross which was placed there by the men of the surrounding parishes in 1950.

From the brow of Tory Hill, on a clear day, you can see five counties. There is, to the Waterford side, a section of rock which is in the form of an armchair, out on the very edge of the hill. This we were told was called Cromwell's chair because it is said he came up the hill to view the surrounding territory. There could be truth in this as it is well known that not far from there his men caused terrible slaughter, but that is another story.

14

KILKENNY CATS

My father, God be good to him, was a great Kilkenny supporter and he used to frighten the lives out of us when he climbed up a rickety old timber ladder to place the black and amber flag on the chimney. When I think of it now, it must have looked funny, he on the ladder, brave and heroic, as he wasn't fond of heights and distrusted the ladder, and our Mam and a swarm of us children gathered around the foot of it, urging him to be careful or sucking our breaths as it wobbled when he climbed over the lip of the roof onto the tiles. Afterwards, when the black and amber flew valiantly in the wind and he had commended my mother for her fine needlework on the flag, he sometimes would laugh with us and say, 'Isn't it well ye don't come from a mixed marriage?' It was later we came to realise what he was laughing at.

A 'mixed marriage' in south Kilkenny usually has nothing at all to do with religion, class or creed. No, it is when one partner is from County Kilkenny and one from County Waterford. There are many such marriages evident now on either side of the River Suir. You need no census to identify them, for in the summer months you will see that on one gate pier the blue and white of Waterford flutters in the wind, while on the other pier the black and amber of Kilkenny flutters defiantly back.

Inside the homes there will be playful exchanges during the GAA season, where family members feel free to turn the term 'Kilkenny Cat' or 'Waterford Rat' into a goading insult. It is the same in the schoolyards and sometimes the odd hothead gets into serious trouble. Black eyes are not part of the black and amber.

The naming of Kilkenny people after a cat goes a long way back. Some tell me that it even goes back to when a cat of terrifying proportions, named Banghaisgidheach, was said to live in the county, out in Dearc Fearna (the Dunmore Caves). This cat prowled the land during the time of the Fianna, when many strange and magical creatures were to be found.

If you have ever tried to remove a cat or a kitten from anywhere, against its will, you will understand just how tenacious they can be. Little claws can become lethal weapons and will cling on to the position they wish to hold in defiance of much greater strength. It is no wonder then that, as history moved on, many people associated the men and women who came from Kilkenny with great staying power. To have a man from Ossory beside you in battle was apparently a great boon. My mother, light of heaven to her, used to say it was just a stubborn streak, and we all had it, God help her.

There is a story from long ago, which tells of how two cats of Kilkenny fought, as only cats can, and after a terribly long battle of hissing, scratching and spitting, when the fur finally settled the onlookers found, to their great horror, that only the tails of both cats remained. They had eaten each other, bless us and save us.

This story used to fascinate us as children and we would chant the old rhyme, which is still repeated today.

> There once were two cats of Kilkenny
> Each thought there was one cat too many
> So they fought and they fit
> And they scratched and they bit
> 'Til (excepting their nails
> And the tips of their tails)
> Instead of two cats there weren't any.

Many stories told to us had this sort of ending and we never knew which story was a parody on the other. There was the story of the tiger which chased his own tail around and around a tree until he turned into a lump of butter, which delighted us also.

Another story from legend tells how, '*Fado, fado*' (long ago), an army of resident cats from Kilkenny met and battled with an army of cats from the rest of Ireland. The battle took place before the saints came to convert us and maybe tied to the legend of Banghaisgidheach in the Dunmore Caves. One ending to this story says that all the cats killed each other until only one remained and that one was killed by a man who never wanted to see such a terrible happening again.

Well, somehow the cat population of Ireland and Kilkenny renewed itself for, as they say, 'The cat came back' and during the years of occupation by the British other stories regarding the cats of the city and county emerged.

The first such story was based on a time when some Hessians (soldiers of German origin) were part of the British forces in Kilkenny and having time on their hands, they amused themselves tormenting misfortunate cats. They tied two cats by their tails and slung them over a washing line and then proceeded to make bets on which cat would survive the fight which ensued, as the cats sought to gain their freedom. Apparently betting was strictly forbidden by army regulations, but murder and torture were permitted.

Well, the soldiers were alarmed when one of their officers was seen approaching and quick as a wink one of them made a swipe with his sword and cut the tails. The cats, finding that they were free, ran for their lives and the dangling remains of their tails flopped to the ground. The officer, knowing well that something had been the centre of the soldier's attention, asked what had happened. A clever young soldier pointed to the remains of the cats' tails, which still seemed to squirm on the ground. Then he told him the fantastic story of how two cats were fighting and, try as they would, they hadn't been able to separate them and, horror of horrors, they had eaten each other down to the tips of their tails.

People at that time were superstitious and believed in sorcery and witches and, as everyone knows, witches had cats and it was as well not to have anything to do with cats. Kilkenny's most famous witch, Alice Kyteler came under suspicion not only for having four dead husbands but she also owned a cat. Aren't we well removed now from all that nonsense, thank heaven?

Another story from the military tells how Cromwell's soldiers dispatched all the cats they found in Kilkenny. It seems to be just a variation on the cats over the wire tale.

Growing up as a 'Kilkenny Cat' was grand. Our sporting teams were hailed as 'The Cats' and we would often hear Mícheal Ó Hehir, that famous radio commentator, cry out in praise of them 'And Eddie Keher for the black and amber bends, lifts and strikes and sends the ball over the bar putting "The Cats" ahead once again'.

The inhabitants of Kilkenny seem content with the name 'The Cats', as far as I can see, and foster the traits of tenacity and endurance in their young men and women.

15

THE WEASEL'S
FUNERAL

There was a story my father used to tell about a man from Aylwardstown who was going home one moonlit night. He was whistling softly to himself as he stepped out on the road. He had not drunk any drink except for a mug of buttermilk, taken at Kilaspy, where he was making arrangements for the slaughter of some pigs.

He took the road easy from there through Ballinamona and out through the Mile Post. The sky was bright with moon and stars by the time he turned off for Scartnamore and, as he was coming down by a place called Donovan's Mill, he thought he saw a movement near the bend of the road ahead of him. He stepped on to the grassy verge, as any sensible man would do, and blinked a few times before he could see the movement again.

The hair on the back of his neck stood on end and he backed himself in against an oak tree by the side of the ditch. The roadway, just a little bit clear of the bend now, seemed to be moving, undulating if you like, and the movement was coming in a wave towards him.

There was a scratching and scritching sound of many nailed feet with the odd squeal or hiss, and every so often a soft bark resounding in the quiet of the night. In the front of the moving throng four strong young weasels bore, on high, the body of a weasel of venerable age. His colouring looked silver-grey in the moonlight, and by the loll of his head you could see he was no longer for this world.

Without a sound, the man removed his cap and bowed his head in silent prayer. Whether the prayer was for the passing of the king weasel or for his own safety was never made clear.

He stood there many minutes while this strange funeral procession moved along within touching distance of the toes of his brogues. There were weasels of every sort and size and all in abject mourning for their dead king, for indeed he must have been a king to have such a huge turnout. The man told later how, on either side of the passing mourners, and coming behind, were weasels which appeared to be keeping control and order among the mourning creatures. What do we know at all? All God's creatures have their own customs and traditions.

When the last animal had finally passed him by, and the rustling and scratching of many paws died away, he stayed quiet for a long while. He strained his eyes to see where they left the road and disappeared through a gap to make their way across the fields towards the high ground.

The scent of musk lingered on the night air, and why wouldn't it, with so many of the creatures passing him by so close, and it a warm night.

It was with very careful quiet steps he continued on his journey until he called in at Kirwan's Sheanti, at the butt of the hill, in Scartnamore. There he had more than buttermilk to drink let me tell you.

Officially there are no weasels in Ireland but instead there are stoats. They are blamed for sucking eggs, stealing chicks, eating mice and voles, and I have seen one take down a medium-size rabbit and haul it away.

They are strangely handsome creatures with chestnut brown coats and a creamy white blaze down the chest and stomach. They were associated with old, otherworld stories in ancient times, and maybe there is more to the culture of these animals than any of us understand now.

At some stage the word weasel became a derogatory term when applied to humans. 'He was a right little weasel.' I suppose if they had said, 'He was a right little stoat' it wouldn't sound half so wicked. Stoats they may be, but if the Irish want to call them weasels then weasels they are.

16

STORIES FROM CASTLECOMER

The folk tales from the Castlecomer area make grim telling but need to be told. These accounts are from the past and the inhabitants today honour the men, women and children who suffered and survived so much hardship. They acknowledge the lives lost to the mines and the courage of their ancestors in a wonderful interactive exhibition area in their new Discovery Park.

According to old records, coal was taken from the earth on the Castlecomer Plateau prior to the 1600s. The arrival, around the mid-1600s, of the Wandesforde family into the area, when they were given the land by the then Lord Deputy of Ireland Thomas Wentwort, saw the start of iron-ore mining and when the ore was spent they mined anthracite coal.

The people of Castlecomer have, since its foundation, been hardworking and industrious. They have also been hounded and harried at all sorts of levels. Castlecomer was destroyed on many occasions by invaders. You would think that they were far enough away from coasts and main cities to be safe but Castlecomer seems to have been like a giant honeypot which had to be attacked and broken open by different people down through the centuries.

But it was a town which refused to play the lie-down-and-die game. A strong and resilient people rebuilt and rebuilt again and again. They survived Vikings, Normans, Cromwell, famine and war. They worked in the black darkness of the mines and clogged their lungs with the black dust. This dust they brought home in their clothing and in every pore of their bodies. So much dust clung to them that the paths they trod when homeward bound became black with the fall of coal dust from their clothing.

At the mouth of the tunnel in the Deerpark mines a shrine to Our Lady, the Blessed Mother, was erected and it became the custom for the miners to stop there and pray for a few minutes before they went into the bowels of the earth. Sure, wouldn't you do it yourself, if you spent your days in dread and danger from so many things? I am sure many stopped briefly again as they emerged into daylight at the end of shift, safe once more from shifting earth, rock collapses, gas or injuries. This statue is now set up on the Castlecomer to Clogh road on a plot of ground kindly donated by the Boran family.

Each miner had a brass disc with his own number on it. This was left in the office. They took this disc with them every time they went down the mine and replaced it on the hook when they came back up in the evening. If a disc was missing then the alarm was raised for it meant that someone was unaccounted for. Sometimes a tired and weary man, maybe with a blinding headache after the day in the poor air below, would forget to hang up his disc and there would be holy murder.

They learned quickly to carry their lunch in tin boxes as the rats ran in packs down below. They carried their tea in bottles and were glad to drink it cold when it was time to break. Seamus Walsh, in his book *In the Shadow of the Mines*, tells how the old miners never took any notice of the rats except if the rats started to head up out of the mine. Then they would quickly follow them as they believed that the rats were aware of danger below ground before men. It seems that they were often right.

Seamus also tells how the miners hung their lunch tins, tied with twine, from the roof of the tunnel, but some of the rats quickly learned to chew through the twine. Down dropped the box and out fell the lunch which made a substantial meal for a rat. The miners always feared the disease carried in the urine of rats known as Weil's Disease.

For a long time life in the mining community became a vicious circle, which seemed to close off the minds of the inhabitants to the dream or possibility of any other lifestyle. It was as though they were frozen in time and when a child was born into the community, if it was a boy then he was destined for the mines and if a girl she would be a miner's wife.

They lived in a world ruled by hooters, darkness, dust and the gleam of coal in a fresh seam.

The women tell tales of how, in the early dark days, their men-folk would come home with their clothing caked with the black dust and because it was the only set of clothing they had, it had to be ready for the morning as the dawn broke again. The men would sit in one tin bath, and in another their clothing would be washed and re-washed, dried and beaten in an effort to make them wearable for another day. Sometimes it was not possible to get the clothing dry and the men would don the still wet clothing to go to work in the early hours of the morning.

There is one account by a miner's daughter where she tells that her father once came home with his clothing frozen stiff and crackling with the frost. Bless us and save us, if that was now he would have been

rushed to hospital and treated for hypothermia but I don't believe the word had been invented then. They were great people to survive.

Another tells of how, as a child, she would walk the black path with her father and he would have to stop many times because he could not get his breath and she did not understand that he had the miner's disease of silicosis in the lungs, but thought he was admiring the view and delaying.

It is hard to think now that people lived and worked in such terrible conditions. However, that is what their lives were, backbreaking work and coming home too exhausted to even talk or think sometimes, only to be woken too soon again by the hooter from the mine.

Many young men who started work in the mines grew old too fast from the unrelenting toil and once they sustained an injury or began to have difficulty breathing they were unable to continue.

They used candles stuck into balls of clay to give them light while they hacked and gouged out the coal. They had to pay for the packs of candles they used. Imagine the poor men, barely earning enough to keep body and soul together, and the company would charge them for the candles. Heart-breaking is the only word I can give.

If a miner sustained a cut or graze while extracting the coal he had no recourse to first aid or any such thing so they found their own way of dealing with small injuries. They dripped the hot candle wax on to the wound to seal it until they could get their shift finished and head back up above ground to have it seen to.

Even in these dire conditions the men had a sense of humour. Human nature is wonderful. There is a story told about a man who sustained a broken leg when a huge boulder came down on him in the tunnel where he was working. The men with him managed to get him free but had to haul him back through a three foot high tunnel to get him to safety. As they were hauling him along with great difficulty, the man on the plank of timber, knowing very well how hard it was, asked would it help if I put out the good leg and walked it along? Needless to say he was told that he better keep it in or he would have two broken legs.

While the men worked below ground, lying on their sides in wet and narrow cramped tunnels, which were sometimes little wider than their own shoulder span, the women had different work.

They were great women by all accounts and were hardworking and industrious on a scale never seen since.

They could turn their hand to anything, bless them. They reared large families in terrible conditions and sure, there was no such thing as contraception then. When people live on the brink of existence the need to bring new life into the world seems to be stronger. The women in the house of a miner went out to work for farmers, on the land and in the houses, took in washing, cooked and still reared their children. They would come home, weary from harvesting potatoes but glad that they carried enough potatoes to feed the family that evening, and perhaps a gallon of milk or half-dozen eggs as payment.

There are accounts of how the women in the Castlecomer area, long ago, used to carry their baskets and *bresnas* (bundles) of firewood upon their heads in the same manner as some African tribeswomen still carry their loads. They had a name for the bag in which they carried the potatoes on their heads, it was a *práiscín*. The same name applied to an apron in which they gathered the tops off the grasses (*tráithníns*). The bundles they took home they dried and beat with sticks to get the seeds. The dried seeds were sold to a Mr Fennessy in High Street in Kilkenny, who then sold them on to the farmers for more than he paid the women, of course. No wonder some of the farmers didn't want the women coming on to their fields. But anyway the grass grew plentiful by the side of the roads then.

The main work the women took on was a side product of miner's work. There was a way of using the coal slack or dust which was known as tempering the Culm. The culm was mixed with yellow clay and water and the women and old or injured men would make this mixture into what they called bums or bombs. This mixture was made like we would mix cement these days, for every eight measures of culm there was one measure of clay. It was measured out onto a patch of ground and then the yellow clay added and just enough water to make it become sticky.

Once the mixture was right it was tramped upon or 'danced' on for a long time or until it became so sticky that it was hard to lift the boots from it. It was also done beneath the hooves of animals, horses, jennets or donkeys went around and around in big circles. Sometimes the animals drew a heavy grindstone round and round over the culm. It was normal to cover the eyes of the animal so that they would not get dizzy if the circle was small.

Those who made the culm balls or bums gathered fistfuls of this mixture and with each hand they could make these round cakes or bums so fast that your eye could hardly follow the movement. Years and years of practice gave them skills that earned for the poor families an extra little ration. Sometimes these bums were paid for 'in kind' and a woman might come home with a half-dozen eggs or some vegetables or potatoes for the dinner when she did this work. But they also had to do this work to keep their own fires going.

There is a story about a poor old man who was injured and could no longer work and he spent his time sitting by the fire making bums. His brother was outside, working in the yard, when the British soldiers came and asked his whereabouts. Without thinking, his brother just said that he was inside by the fire, making bums. Well, that caused a scatter I can tell you. Next thing the door was banged open and the poor old man by the fire found himself on the wrong side of an array of bayonets. Needless to remark, the soldiers, when they realised that 'bums' were not the same as 'bombs', were not amused.

It took a long time before conditions improved for the miners. They eventually managed to organise themselves enough to get a union going. A man called Nixie Boran was a leader in this and he went so far as to go to Russia to see how they ran their unions. The poor man was arrested when he came home, such was the fear the governments of the time had about Communism spreading. The miners stood with Nixie and his companions in an effort to obtain a fair wage for the miners. It appears that none of those who opposed justice for the miners ever went down a mine in their lives, but were happy to say they were not to get a fair wage.

One of the hardest stories is that the Catholic Church, instead of looking after their downtrodden flock, saw fit to side with the company and the government in their condemnation of the miners. The results could have been so different if the Church of the time had spoken out against the terrible conditions the miners had to suffer.

They did put their hands out to take up collections from the miners to build schools and churches for people who worked like slaves and faced shortened lives from the miners' disease of the lungs. Ah but sure, weren't their feet warm and snug and not a chick or a child with any of them?

The Roman Catholic Bishop of Ossory at that time, Dr Collier, saw fit to accuse the poor men of working for the devil and threatened them with excommunication at a time when their need was greatest. There was little Christianity in the voice which raged in the church against the miners and when the bishop ordered all present to renew their baptismal vows or be damned he pushed too far. The rule by fear was broken when the men walked out of the church on the heels of Nixie Boran, leaving the bishop fuming in a stew of his own making.

Well, after that it was time for things to change. The change came slowly but surely. The wages were increased eventually but not by very much. New machinery was purchased to increase productivity but it did ease the workload of the miners below ground. The tunnels became larger. New systems were developed and washing facilities and lockers were provided for the miners. This eased the workload on the women as well but for a lot of miners it was too little too late.

Down through the years many lives were lost in the mines and through working in the mines. In the 300 plus years that the mines operated it is said that not as many were lost in Castlecomer as in other mining areas. Perhaps the prayer to Our Lady of the Miners helped.

The mines in Castlecomer closed on 31 January 1969.

The compilation of this piece was made possible with the help of many people in the Castlecomer area including Seamus Walsh, author of In the Shadows of the Mines. *Mary Morrissey, Castlecomer librarian; Aisling Kelly, Kilkenny Library; John's Quay; the staff at Discovery Park; Maline Campbell; and Mary Phelan.*

I was assured by many people including Willie Joe Mealy, from Clogh, that the people of Castlecomer did have times of laughter and good humour and it was not always dark and desperate.

17

FOLK TALES FROM CROSSPATRICK

Stories about Fionn McCumhaill and Oisín were popular when we were young and we often wondered about these wonderful heroes who were known as The Fianna. They were, according to the tales we were told, huge fine men, bless them. Well, isn't it a great thing to know, at last, that they were all well fed and catered for in the upper reaches of County Kilkenny.

Let *The Annals of the Four Masters* say what they like, we now have the truth of it. By great good fortune I met with a lovely young lady, named MaryAnn Vaughan, who regaled me with all the details I needed to bring this matter to your attention.

A story in the Schools Collection for the Folklore Commission from this area was submitted by M. Grady, from Margaret Dwyer, and it read as follows:

> In John Bowes Rath Oisín's gold is said to be buried. A good few years ago people named Morrisey dreamt there was gold there. They went to the priest who told them to dig for it, but while digging a dog would appear. He told them not to be frightened but to stay on digging. They went and dug and the dog appeared. They were so frightened that they ran home. Then they told the priest about it and he said, 'Uh ye are good, there won't be a Morrisey in Eark yet and they'll leave it begging. These Morriseys are living in Johnstown now.' [Eark refers to the parish of Erke.]

MaryAnn told me that the 'John Bowe's Rath', referred to above, is where her family live now, in the townland of Rathosheen:

> The land that the rath is on no longer belongs to our house but to our neighbours but you can see the rath from our window and it is where my brothers and myself would spend all our time playing. There is another large rath in the same townland – to the south. It is said that Oisín lived in our rath, which is a fairly substantial rath, but when he died the fairies carried him and put him in the other rath.
>
> Eugene O'Curry has it in his book that there were two fine stones that marked the grave of Oisín in that rath but that the place was dug up several years ago by money-dreamers and the stones carried away by some evil man who couldn't care less about the rath or the grave. It is said that the man was cursed for disturbing the grave of Oisín. He died soon afterwards although he wasn't very old.

She also assured me that there is a townland called Rathoscar, which was named for Oisín's son, Oscar, just the other side of Fertagh, and Sui Finn (the Seat of Fionn), Oisín's father, is on the Spa Hill.

To further convince me of Kilkenny's claim on Oisín there was the story of how Crosspatrick got its name. St Patrick, it is said, came often to that area for the sole purpose of conversing with Oisín and his friend Caílle mac Rónáin. It seems that St Patrick enjoyed the old stories about the Fianna and held secret hopes of converting the two famous men to Christianity before they died.

While he was there one day, he was giving thanks to God for the great chance he had to be there in the company of the last men of the Fianna and he knelt down at the place where the paths crossed and, lo and behold, he was so hot with his prayer that his knees melted the stone beneath them and the pattern of his knees was to be seen there ever after. That is why this grand little spot is called Crosspatrick.

Well, after hearing all that local information I gave the whole matter some serious thought and it occurred to me that when Fionn, who was Oisín's father, was a young lad wasn't he reared on the side of the Slieve Bloom mountains by the his Aunt Bodhmall who was a druidess, and the warrior woman Liath Luachra?

Isn't it well known that in the time before counties were so called that whoever ruled the territory of Ossory also held sway over the same mountains? Well, Fionn and the Fianna and, of course, young Oisín would have known that area like the back of their hands, and the Slieve Bloom mountains were only a stone's throw away from Crosspatrick, especially for a warrior of the Fianna.

Ah, I am thinking that those monks who wrote the same Annals didn't know much about young warriors or indeed the old ones either. I wonder if they were in the habit of 'tidying' things up a bit.

Gods and Fighting Men by Lady Gregory contains an account of a supposed conversation between St Patrick and Oisin. It is titled Oisin and Patrick The Arguments. If we were to take this to heart it would appear that St Patrick and poor Oisin were not content together but were always wrangling and Oisin is constant in his complaint of being hungry and putting up with the presence of the monks.

'My grief that I ever took baptism; it is little credit I got by it, being without food, without drink, doing fasting and praying.'

18

ST NICHOLAS AND JERPOINT

Jerpoint was an important place in medieval times. It was frequented by nobles and knights as well as merchants. Monks from two different orders set up homes there, one taking over from the other. In 1160 Domnall Mac Gillapadraig, King of Osraige, set up a monastery there for the Benedictine Order. Twenty years later the poor Benedictines got the shove and Donogh O'Donoghoe Mac Gillapatraig, who was now in charge of Osraige, installed the Cistercian Order of monks and proceeded to construct the Abbey.

Jerpoint Abbey was a wonderful place with sufficient lands around it to make it self-supporting although, down through the centuries that followed, many additions were made which were probably funded by the powerful families in Osraige. The architecture of the present-day ruins show many different styles and the sculptured cloister arcade, with its unique carvings, is famous.

The monks prospered in Jerpoint until the Dissolution of the Monasteries by Henry VIII. It must have broken the hearts of its incumbents when their abbot, Oliver Grace, had to hand over the beautiful Abbey to the forces of the king. It came under the control of James Butler, the 9th Earl of Ormond, in 1541.

I suppose that it could have been worse for it was still a much sought after site by rich and famous as a burial place. One of the earliest famous people to be interred there was Felix O'Dullany, Bishop of Osraige, in 1202.

There are many stories told about Jerpoint Abbey but a more intriguing story is told about the nearby town of Newtown Jerpoint. It is now known as the 'lost town' for it has disappeared into the mists of time. Newtown Jerpoint was a very busy town which controlled an important crossing place over the River Nore. It had a toll bridge and all the usual businesses which grew up around such strategically placed crossings. They had many dwelling houses, which were homes to tanners, brewers, and those who worked in the local woollen mill. In fact, it was so busy that it was necessary to have a court house to keep order. This is not surprising when you hear that, at one time, there were as many as fourteen taverns situated close to the crossing.

Even though the Abbey was just down the road, Newtown Jerpoint had its own church, which was used by many of those who were passing through and had no wish to get caught up in the work of the monks. The Norman knights, on their way to the Crusades, were in the habit of using this little church and so it was no wonder that eventually something unusual would be brought back to this church by some devout knights.

Religious fervour was stirred up by the prospect of going on a Crusade to the Holy Land, to save Christendom from the Infidels. Now, I am sure that many a knight, and much less his squire, had any notion at all who the Infidels were. To many it was to be a grand, chivalrous adventure, taking them away from all the local strife and maybe gaining for them spiritual rewards, not available at home.

Well, two such knights who passed through Newtown Jerpoint must have had religious fervour aplenty for they came back home with more than spiritual rewards, as we know them. They carried with them, in a specially constructed casket, what they claimed to be the holy remains of St Nicholas, Bishop of Myra. They were well pleased with themselves, I expect, and soon after all the acclamation and surprise died down didn't they become famous in their own way.

The remains they had brought home, which they assured all and sundry were the true relics of St Nicholas, had to be interred and this took place in the graveyard of the little church, now called after St Nicholas. On the memorial slab covering the final resting place of the saint's relics, an engraving shows the figure of a religious man with the very obvious depiction of two knight's heads, one behind each shoulder.

If this story is true then we should be giving much more respect to that grave in Jerpoint. The story of St Nicholas is not just the Santa Claus story, with which everyone is familiar. Yes, there is the story of how he threw the purses of gold in through the window of a poor man's home to enable his daughters to have dowries and not be disgraced before the town, but St Nicholas was a mighty saint compared to many others.

He was born in Patara, a city west of Myra (called Demre now), which is in Turkey. His parents were Theophanes and Nonna and they were prosperous, but they both died of the plague when Nicholas was in his teens. Nicholas was left a lot of money on his parents' death and this is where the legend of the gold purses through the window started. He gave away his money and joined his uncle, who was also named Nicholas, and was an Abbot in a nearby monastery.

The story of how St Nicholas became Bishop of Myra is strange. When the resident bishop passed away the religious could not agree who was to be the next bishop. Then the oldest and wisest cleric dreamed that a voice called him and said that on the following morning a young man called Nicholas would come in through the city gate during matins and he was the one who should be Bishop of Myra. Well, that is how it happened.

Apparently Nicholas was a great man and worked many, many miracles, protecting children, saving lives, calming storms, feeding a starving city full of people with blessed corn and appearing in answer to calls for help. These were the miracles which took place while he was still living but since his death miracles, through his intervention, have been recorded all around the world.

The most astounding story about St Nicholas is still unfolding. When he died in the year AD 343 he was laid to rest in Myra and shortly after it was noticed that what was called 'manna' appeared to be flowing from the tomb. This blessed manna brought many cures to those who came for it.

Then the unthinkable happened. War came to Myra and it is said that a group of sailors, fearing that the blessed tomb would be desecrated, took away the remains of St Nicholas to the City of Bari, in Italy, where it was once again enshrined, and the manna still came from the original tomb and now appeared also in Bari.

Now, things were very chaotic all across Europe at this time and the Norman knights were everywhere, as indeed were the sailors who took them on their Crusades. Several ships put in at Myra with the intention of removing the relics of St Nicholas and there is a story that one group of Crusaders who had come through Venice found not one casket in the crypt of St Nicholas's Cathedral, but three. One was of the uncle of St Nicholas, who was also called Nicholas, and one was of Bishop Theodore. Well, in the excitement of the find it is said that the real St Nicholas's remains were damaged, and when you remember that he had been dead since AD 343 and it was now 1169, it is little wonder that they were quickly reduced to smithereens.

The story then says that the holy remains were taken to Bari and to Venice separately. Now, if we remember our two Norman knights from Jerpoint, perhaps they were among those who removed the relics and, accidentally by design, found themselves in possession of some of them, which they duly and with reverence placed in a casket of their own and brought it back to Newtown Jerpoint.

That should be the end of the legend, but there is a further part which historians like to point out. It is said that a French family known as de Frainets, also Crusading knights, who had lands in Thomastown in County Kilkenny, took the opportunity, when they were being forced out of Bari, to appropriate the relics of St Nicholas. These sacred relics they protected as they retreated back through France and eventually had to take ship back to Ireland. This, according to many, is the true legend of how the remains of St Nicholas came to be buried in Newtown Jerpoint cemetery.

Perhaps some of the relics were carried back to Ireland and are buried here. Maybe our ancestors and the Norman knights didn't know about the appearance of the 'manna' on the tomb of the saint. If they did they would surely have tried to keep it safe from our Irish weather.

The feast day of St Nicholas is celebrated in most countries across Europe on 6 December.

Forensic tests, carried out at the request of The Vatican, in the 1950s, deemed the relics in Venice and Bari to be from the same person. I can find no trace of anyone ever having the relics in Newtown Jerpoint graveyard checked.

Further information regarding St Nicholas and his miracles can be found on a website called St Nicholas Centre, www.stnicholascentre.org.

19

Shape~Changing in Ossory

I know you are already smiling when you read the title but let me tell you I am not referring to political shape throwing – sure, that would take more than one story.

There are many references in old documents, down through the ages, to certain people who were able to change shape or leave their bodies to become another creature, while the body lay inert and apparently life-less where they left it. They usually left the body in a safe place so that their return would be easy and unnoticed. Sometimes, unfortunately, a relative or another, not knowing, would find the vacated body and assume it was only fit for burial. Well, once they buried the body there could be no return and the person was forced to remain in whatever shape he or she had assumed, for the rest of their life.

One story suggests that St Patrick was very annoyed with some people in Ossory when they, through pure blackguarding, began to howl like wolves when he was trying to teach them about Christianity. Now, knowing full well the antics some people can get up to I think there may be a grain of truth in this story. Well, anyway St Patrick found it hard to be a saint all the time, as we know from other stories, and he said to himself if they think baying like wolves is great fun then they might as well know the rest of the animal. Whatever he said or did had a terrible effect and thereafter many of those who lifted their faces to the sky and made fun of the saint found that they were often in the shape of wolves, whether they liked it or not, and this trait was passed on to their descendants.

According to a mention in a very old document known as *Lebor na hUidre or Leabhar na Uidhre* (Book of the Dun Cow) written when Ireland was young, shape changing and resurrection were discussed. The writer of the book Máel Muire MacCétechair says that the Resurrection 'shall be different for them all'. He is also specific in mentioning the transformation of a man into a wolf. So it would appear that it was generally accepted that this was possible and did happen.

The romantic part of me would like to believe that when the Tuatha de Dannan began to withdraw from the land of Eiru into the invisible world, that some of them remained mortal and intermarried with the Milesians who came to settle here. These then would still have retained their supernatural powers and shape changing was not a problem for them.

It was often mentioned to us as children that in medieval history An Iarla Mór (The Great Earl), Gearoid Mór Fitzgerald, could shape change whenever he wished and his daughter Margaret, the infamous Countess of Ormond was also believed to be an adept of such arts.

Ossory is again mentioned in connection with man/wolf transformations by Giraldus Cambrensis. Now, I don't know about anyone else but I have always had my doubts about that man and have stood by his tomb in St David's in Wales and told him so myself.

Giraldus didn't think much of Ireland or its residents, but he was neither a soldier nor a knight, so he was content to spend time eating and drinking as he travelled the length and breadth of the land in the wake of Strongbow. He was, as they say, a 'pass remarkable' sort of man and this did not go unnoticed by the people of Ossory.

Someone may have fed him more than food for he tells a story of how in Ossory there were always two people, a man and a woman, living their lives in the shape of wolves: each couple remained so for seven years, at the end of which time, if they lived so long, they were permitted to return to their home and another pair took their place. Giraldus blamed this on a curse pronounced against the people of Ossory by St Natalis. St Natalis was the son of a Munster king, and he died in AD 564. The kingdom of Munster extended well into

Ossory at that time so we can't put his curse down to the Waterford/ Kilkenny antipathy of the GAA followers. He is the patron saint of Kilmanagh in west Kilkenny.

I have always had a fondness for wolves and their care for their own pack. Once, a long time ago, I dreamed that a wolf came hurrying from a great distance to warn me that a grandchild was ill and I never questioned it but woke and lit a candle and prayed. In the morning when I checked with the family it was indeed so. Perhaps there is more to transformation and other lives than we know.

20

FRENEY THE ROBBER

There are many versions of this tale but I will tell it to you as it came to me. It was part of my childhood. Tory Hill, which was within cycling distance, was reputed to be one of Freney's haunts and to listen to my father and his generation talk about him you would swear that they knew Freney personally. This seems to be normal where local folk tales are handed on.

The ancestors of this Freney were of a noble line with links to the kings of France through the 1st Duke of Normandy marrying Princess Gisla, daughter of King Charles of France. The name took many turns down through the centuries, going from De Frayne to De Fraxinis, D'Alfrain, De Faulk, Ffrench and, lastly, to the gentleman robber known as Franey or Freney who was the scourge of the aristocracy in County Kilkenny and surrounding counties in the 1740s.

His name was James Freney and, though from a noble line, his ancestors had long ago lost their acquired land. His parents were well respected and in the employ of a Mr Robbins who was a big landlord with an estate in Ballyduff, a few miles distant from Inistioge.

James was a likeable young lad and the Robbins family included him in the education provided for those who worked for them. They probably thought he would be a good addition to the running of the estate once he came to manhood, and that his parents, their valued servants, would be delighted as well. They probably were, the poor misguided people, and their vision of the future more than likely saw young James wealthy and prosperous, on account of this education, so that he could take care of them when they were no longer able to work themselves.

Ah but the dreams and plans of others were not going to be the path young James would follow.

He was fond of the good life, provided for him by his parents and mentors, but showed little willingness to work as hard as his parents. The life of the gentry was more suited to his ideas.

There was little in the way of entertainment for young people, in those times but James amused himself as best he could, sporting and gambling with the local young men. He was fond of horses and didn't mind working with them but he wasn't keen at all about cleaning and polishing. Then there were young ladies around as well and in no time at all James became involved with a young woman. Sure, weren't the young ladies flocking around this handsome young rascal?

However, he had just turned twenty-one when he married this young lady, who happened to have a small dowry, and they crossed the River Suir and set up home in the City of Waterford. Home is probably not the correct word as they purchased a public house and were in business in no time. She was a grand comely lass and he was charming and forceful so it looked like they were set up to be comfortable for ever.

They should have been but James blithely overlooked the need to be on good terms with his competitors and the authorities were soon notified that this interloper had come across the river and set up his business without let or leave. Sure, things are ever the same between the inhabitants of south Kilkenny and Waterford City. It was pointed out that he was not a freeman of the city so he shouldn't be conducting trade of any sort in Waterford. This was the start of a decline in the barely born fortunes of James and his new wife. They had no choice but to sell up, at a loss, and return to his home place between Innistioge and Thomastown.

It must have been hard on them to admit defeat after their grand exit to make their own way in the world. They lived on credit as the dowry money was now gone and James was not working. It was inevitable that he should fall into bad company and he just hanging around the countryside, still playing the well-to-do young bucko. God help his poor young wife, she must have been scalded with his airs and graces. It is likely that she got some form of employment herself in the end, as women then were very resourceful in keeping body and soul together.

The bad company James fell in with was John Reddy, who lived nearby, and he was a member of the notorious Kellymount Gang. His first robbery was under the wing of John Reddy but because of his reckless delight in the deeds they perpetrated he was held in high regard by the gang members. Sure, in no time at all they were calling him 'Captain Freney' and he drew to himself his own gang. His right-hand man was James Bolger, another rascal and what a team they made.

Some say, that as a kindness to his parents and because he was still well liked, he was asked to work again for the Robbins family, this time as a groom. This meant that he now 'lived in' over the stables where he had charge over the horses both of the family and the visiting gentry. Sure, this suited James very well. He was free at night to roam the countryside and knew what guests were being entertained and what houses would be empty and open to robbery.

He is reputed to have been generous with his ill-gotten gains. James always had a soft heart when it came to robbing the ladies and would often return their jewellery if they were upset. During his mad escapades of relieving his victims of their purse he always made sure they had enough left to them so they could get home. This kind of good deed became his hallmark and endeared him to the ordinary people. Freney appears to have treated the whole outlaw business as some kind of grown up prank.

He also had an education which, in his later years, enabled him to put pen to paper in the form of his own autobiography, *Life and Adventures of James Freney*. It also gave him the ability to write ransom notes to his wealthy victims. Sure, you can't beat the bit of education when it comes to highway robbery.

James was not as serious about robbing as the rest of the gang and it is said that in a foolish attempt to rob a neighbouring landlord,

who was a frequent visitor to his current master's establishment, that Freney carelessly let his face be seen and he was immediately recognised by his victim. Once that happened there was no going home to the comfort of his own bed, so James Frayne was perforce outside the law and on the run.

There were many people willing to give sanctuary to young James and he availed of all the help he could get. In this way he managed to establish a grand network of willing helpers and spies throughout the county and indeed into the neighbouring territories of Carlow, Wicklow and Wexford as well.

The network of spies was important for people are given to chatting and talking while going about their own business and so would often hear that a consignment of goods were being sent between towns and cities or that there was to be a ball or a gathering in a big house where the gentry would be wearing their gold and jewellery, without much regard for safety.

Young James had a quick mind and could set up a plan of attack with very little notice. He was often abroad under cover of darkness to come upon an unwary traveller and relieve them of their purse. It was a time when people had to journey without benefit of our modern-day conveniences and many a weary mile had to be walked or made on horseback or with a donkey and trap as a mode of conveyance. This was especially so with travelling craftsmen who plied their trade from village to village or in some cases from farmhouse to farmhouse.

Well, the story of the night James Freney came upon a travelling tailor runs as follows. The poor tailor had received small money for a set of everyday wear at a farmhouse and was on his way, with hope in his heart, to a more prosperous landlord. He trudged along, by the light of the moon, planning in his head how he would persuade the more wealthy family to give him some work. Thinking about a decorative trim for the gown of the lady of the house, he was taken completely by surprise when who should come out of the shadows but the bould Freney. The following words are attributed to Freney himself:

> As by Thomastown I took my way
> I met a tailor dressed most gay,
> I boldly bid him for to stan'
> Thinking he was some gentleman,
> And it's oh! bold Captain Freny –
> Oh! bold Freny oh!
> 'Upon his pockets I laid hold –
> The first thing I got was a purse of gold;
> The next thing I found, which did me surprise,
> Was a needle, thimble and chalk likewise,
> And it's oh! bold Captain Freny-
> Oh! bold Freny oh!
> 'Your dirty trifle I distain' –
> With that I returned him his gold again
> I'll rob no tailor if I can –
> I'd rather ten times rob a man!'
> And it's oh! bold Captain Freny-
> Oh! bold Freny oh!

A very lucky tailor continued gratefully on his way and he now had a story to tell as well when he finally reached his destination. Perhaps this was James Freney's way to make up for the horror inflicted upon another tailor by one of his relatives at a place called Plunket's Glen, near Listerling.

This legend of Budesha Freinagh or Knight de Frayne came to me from Ger Crotty in Portlaw Heritage Centre.

The legend tells of a wicked Knight de Frayne, who abused his power by ill-treating his tenants and terrorising all who came within his reach. A tailor named Plunkett had the misfortune to be hired by this black-hearted wretch to make for him a suit. The suit was to be ready on a certain day but no one knows if it was or not for the Knight de Frayne declared himself unsatisfied with the garment and had the tailor buried alive.

The legend further relates that while this gruesome act was being perpetrated a supernatural voice was heard to exclaim in the air; 'guilfer, guilfer, guilfer'. That is, 'you shall pay for it'. De Franey was startled at the words, and demanded, 'Who shall pay for it?'

When the voice answered, 'Not you but your seventh generation,' De Frayne is reported to have replied laughingly, 'If it is to go so far, the devil may care!'

According to local tradition this doom is believed to have been fearfully fulfilled in the fall of the family from its high estate. It is also said that the descendants of the cruel knight have been haunted by this voice down through the generations. The spot where this atrocity took place is shunned by all. A farmer who once held the land decided to have the cairn removed from the middle of his fields and when his labourers began work they found the tailor's bones and even his scissors and fled in terror. No one dared touch Plunkett's place of entombment thereafter.

To get back to our much more likeable James Freney, the Robber, who was held in much love and affection by those who were down-trodden by the systems in place, at that time. He loved the risk and the chase which followed, by all accounts. There is a story told about how he once was chased by a large number of the sheriff's men and he took to the hills, abandoning his horse as he went. He secreted himself in a sheltered place beneath an overhang of rock and screened by bushes. He could hear the searchers as they spread out across the foot of the hill and he settled himself in, satisfied that they would not stumble across this hideout.

Ah James, it never pays to be so cocksure. He should never have stretched out and closed his eyes for sleep took him and no wonder for he spent most of his nights out on the dark highway plying his trade. Well, he was no sooner asleep than he started to snore. Not just a quiet purr of a snore, not at all, sure it started soft enough then progressed to several snorts and rounded off with a great prolonged hoarse, groaning sound, like a sleeping horse.

You have to understand that in those times there was little or no background noise when you were out and about, especially in the country, for there was no machinery murmuring away anywhere. So into the stillness of the warm summer's day his snores echoed loudly enough to catch the attention of one of the searchers nearby. Quietly the searcher withdrew but marked well the spot where the snores were resounding. He quickly informed the commander of the party and, without a thought, he ordered the men to advance a bit further and then to open fire. Tormented by the long search and aggravated by the escapades of the rascal Freney they needed no second bidding.

Talk about a rude awakening. Only that he remembered where he was in time Freney could have cracked his skull on the over-hanging rock above him and saved them all the trouble of shooting. But when the shooting started he froze in position, knowing that it would be ill luck indeed if he was shot where he lay. Several times the party fired until the officer in charge was certain that no one could possibly be alive after such an assault on the hiding place. No movement from above confirmed this belief and he ordered the men to prepare to return home and two were sent up the hillside to drag out the dead highwayman.

It was with great exultation that the two men approached the hiding place and, sure enough, there they could see the two legs of Freney, sticking out through the ferns and bushes. Below them their companions began to leave and so they hastily grabbed a leg each and hauled out the 'dead' highwayman. Imagine their shock and horror when they came face to face with his pistol. They dropped his legs quickly then, I can tell you, and took to their heels. Freney jumped up and with the agility of a mountain goat was away down the hillside before the searchers fully realised that they had made a big mistake. Freney grabbed the reins of a horse belonging to one of the officers and took off like a shot across country leaving many red faces behind him.

But all good things must come to an end and Freney was nearing the end of his reign. The grand network of spies and helpers sprung a leak. Poor people can be coerced into many things and with the threat of torture or hanging someone was bound to talk.

Some of his gang took the option of betrayal for personal gain. The law then allowed the one who broke silence and gave evidence against his fellow gang member to go free himself. Apparently with the law now nipping at the heels of Freney's gang, betrayal became the norm rather than unusual.

In the final days James Freney and his companion James Bolger were the only ones left and the only ones who trusted each other. Even that seems to have been a mistake. The two highwaymen were proclaimed as 'Tories, Robbers and Rapparees' and they were given the ultimatum that they surrender before August of the year 1748 or they would be charged with high treason. This was different entirely from the charge of highway robbery. High treason meant the death sentence for sure.

To add to their woes some merchants put up a reward of £100 for their capture. To poor people then that was like a gift from heaven. It was time to end the wild career. Freney might be a robber and a highwayman but he was not guilty of treason. Indeed he had not, up to that point, killed anyone at all.

There are two different endings that I know of to this story. One tells that Freney betrayed his companions and in particular James Bolger so that he might gain his own freedom. He had always maintained a good relationship with his old friends since boyhood. Many were now in positions of power and he leaned on their generosity and friendship to secure his freedom.

The other ending says that he was with Bolger when they were discovered. The house in which they were hiding was surrounded by the militia who set it on fire. Given no other choice, they both came out of the house, firing pistols in every direction and managed to escape. Unfortunately James Bolger was wounded as they fled. James Freney in his own autobiography tells how he carried Bolger as far as he was able through woods but in the end Bolger insisted that he leave him and save himself. We have never been told that Freney was untruthful in his life so perhaps this is the true version. Whatever happened, Freney himself escaped and his friend was taken and sentenced to be hanged. Bolger was hanged but his body was taken away that night and never located again.

James Freney got his freedom through the good offices of those whose friendship he had valued all his life. After a period of five or six years lying low, during which time he wrote his autobiography, James Freney was not in the limelight again for a long time.

Somehow he managed to reinvent himself and came to notice again twenty years later as a Tidewaiter, at New Ross Port. This position was like that of a present-day customs officer. He knew all the dodges and so was a valuable employee, at last. He continued to work in New Ross Port until his death which was in 1788. His grave is unmarked, which is a wonder really. Surely, even then, his famous exploits and infamous past was worthy of a headstone and of interest to passing scholars.

Many books have been written which are about, or include mentions of, James Freney. In recent times his autobiography has been republished – The Life and Adventures of James Freney. *However, the account I have given is the stuff of fireside tales in the 1950s.*

21

BALLYKEEFE WOOD

Ballykeefe Wood lies some distance from Kilkenny City as you journey towards Callan. There are many stories concerning Ballykeefe Wood but perhaps the tale of how the wood came to be planted is the strangest one of all.

There was no wood there at one time but a little church occupied a bit of that land at the place called Doorath. Successive repressions saw to the demise of the church. The Rath was there from long before the time when the saints brought Christianity to that part of the world. It is said that the Rath is still occupied and is not a good place to be walking near at the time of the full moon. Music and the sound of merriment have been reported to come from the depths of the earth. Some say that the music is so powerful and soothing that a person who hears it could die from longing to hear it again.

Well, be that as it may, the land was renamed Knocknacarriga and came into the ownership of a man called Walsh. In those times farmers travelled many a long mile to a fair to sell and buy animals. There was a famous fair in Galway which brought in people from far and wide. Mr Walsh decided that his land was a suitable place for rearing sheep and, knowing that the very best creatures would be got at the Sheep Fair in Galway, away he went.

Now, in those times a trip to Galway took more than one day. It was normal to get lodgings somewhere on the way and then again when you reached the outskirts of Galway City. This is what Mr Walsh did and he stayed overnight in a boarding house where many other farmers stayed. In the morning while they were waiting for the fair to start one of the men present began to read from a big book. To own a book then was a great thing entirely and the man was reading aloud to his most attentive audience, for they had nothing else to do yet a while.

Our Mr Walsh was listening contentedly when he suddenly heard mention of Knocknacarriga. He knew full well that it was possible that there was more than one place of that name and the chances of someone mentioning his farm in a book was remote indeed. However, as he listened the man read out that there would be one hundred acres of land planted in County Kilkenny in a place called Knocknacarriga.

Walsh couldn't contain himself any longer and jumped up and declared before all that it couldn't be right for that was his land – hadn't he farmed it man and boy? The man reading the book shook his head and said the book was called *Colmcill's Prophesy* and had never been known to be wrong. St Colmcill was a great saint, as they

all knew. Walsh shook his head and thought to himself that even a saint can be wrong sometimes. The man offered to show him where it was written but it didn't make much difference to Walsh for he never had the benefit of much schooling himself but he could make out the word Knocknacarriga. Doubt now assailed him.

When the fair started he purchased the very best sheep he could afford and set off on the long journey back to the county of Kilkenny. As he walked, Walsh consoled himself with the thought that maybe it was a prophesy for many years later. When he came back home to his little farm, and he herding his new sheep, his distracted wife met him. A man representing the landlord, Lord Desart, had called while he was away and informed her that they would be taking over one hundred acres for planting. So not only was his farm gone now but many another besides. Colmcill's prophesy was right again.

Ballykeefe Wood was planted and a wall built around it. The planting and building of the wall gave employment to many but what was building another man's wall compared to running your own little farm. I expect the sheep found their way to the kitchen table before too long.

Perhaps we should all take a look at Colmcill's prophesy.

22

THE HIGHWAYMAN
FROM BALLYCALLAN

In the early 1800s the people of County Kilkenny were severely oppressed. The same could be said for the rest of Ireland as the Penal Laws were being enforced with renewed brutality since the 1798 rebellion. Kilkenny was held tightly in the grip of the Earl of Ormond and other lords of the land.

The tenant farmers and the landless were suffering many hardships, with many being evicted on the whim of their landlords. The miners in Castlecomer were labouring in dire conditions and, to be honest, Kilkenny was not a good place to be living, unless you were of the gentry.

Well, there is a saying in Ireland 'Come the time, come the man', and they must have believed that in the townland of Ballycallan, for out from the poverty-stricken ranks came a highwayman known locally as Bully Beg. He was no ordinary highwayman either, for he had definite objectives when he took to his new career. He was going to redress the terrible wrongs suffered by his neighbours at the hands of the unscrupulous landlords. So Bully Beg targeted specific persons and places where he knew well he could waylay them.

He was particularly fond of trying for the coin known as the Castlecomer Crown, which was marked 'Payable at Castlecomer Colliery 5 shillings and 5 pence'. A Castlecomer Crown was worth at least 5 shillings of English money and originated, it is said, when the Dowager Countess of Ormond feared that the Spanish silver coins she had amassed would lose their value, so she had them counter-stamped. It was well known that the coins were accepted by merchants in the City of Kilkenny, for all sorts of commodities, and then they would exchange them for their own supply of coal.

He gave up the privilege of living an ordinary miserable life like the rest of the downtrodden and he made a fine hideout in the Ballykeefe Wood. Now, everyone had a good idea where the hideout was but because Bully Beg was robbing the rich to help them, no one was prepared to betray him. Sure, why would they and he probably giving them the only chance of survival they would ever have.

Ballykeefe Wood was on lands owned by John Otway Cuffe, 2nd Early of Desart, and really it was adding insult to injury for Bully Beg to firstly rob the Earl and his visiting gentry and then set up home in the wood on the Desart Court Estate. It was also makings things uncomfortable for the rest of the locals, for they were being rousted out of their miserable homes when their lord's men hunted for Bully Beg.

In desperation the Earl sent his men into the extensive woodlands of Ballykeefe with the command that they should seek out and find the hiding place of this rascally highwayman and blow the whole thing up. Needless to say they never found hair nor hide of the bould Bully Beg.

It was the simplest of a thing that caught Bully Beg in the end. Some people tell how it was that he fell out with a family known as Sherman and that they set him up. Who can tell one way or another now? What is sure is that he was caught in possession of two chickens on the lands owned by the Sherman family at Balleven. He was arrested and charged with the theft of the two miserable chickens. For this heinous crime he was found guilty and sentenced to transportation to Van Dieman's Land.

The mind boggles now to think of it. Two chickens, and to be clapped in irons, placed on board a prison ship and sent to the far side of the world. Sure, we could send a whole fleet of ships there now and the culprits would not come from the poor of the land either.

Well, Bully Beg ended up in Hobart, Tasmania. Life in Tasmania was hard and the convicts, and that is what he was, were set to work the minute they set foot on dry land. The work was anything from breaking stones for roads and buildings, to helping farmers work their small holdings. The military were in charge and Aboriginals were being hunted out of their homeland. If anything, Tasmania was a thousand times worse than life had been back in Ballycallan.

The climate of Tasmania is similar to that of Ireland and snow can cover the hills just like at home so in winter time many prisoners suffered that added hardship. Hunger and ill-treatment was a daily feature of their lives. A prisoner's life was worthless in the eyes of those in power. However, Bully Beg somehow survived the term of his sentence and was once again put on board one of the many sailing ships which plied their way around the world.

Unfortunately, due to the harshness of his treatment and his weakened state, Bully Beg did not survive the journey back around the world to Ireland. Somewhere in the open ocean, with the ship under full sail, the remains of poor Bully Beg slipped without much ceremony into the depths. Perhaps a sea captain said some words to commend him to his Maker. Perhaps the ghost of Bully Beg completed the journey. I would like to believe that his ghost came back, even if it was only to scare the chickens in Balleven.

23

ST FIACHRA
THE GARDENER

Did you know that St Fiachra is the patron saint of gardeners? The fact that he is nearly always depicted with a spade in his hand delights the gardener in me. He was a great man for growing things and was famous for his knowledge of healing herbs. I would like to have known him, but they say he never had any time for women and banned them from the monastery he built in France.

My mother, God rest her, would have said, 'He probably had a bad experience with a woman to make him so contrary but he will make a grand old man.' She could have been right, if the legends are to be believed, but I will tell you about that in a while. First let me tell you about the man himself.

They say that St Fiachra, also known as St Fiacre, was born around the year 590 in the county of Kilkenny. There was, by all accounts, a great fluirse of saints in Ireland at that time and Kilkenny, which was then called Osrithe after Aengus Osrithe, the first king of Ossory, was no exception.

It has also been told that he was descended from one of the High Kings of Ireland called Conn. Whoever his ancestors were he was brought up decent, for, from a young age, he showed a kind and generous nature. He had great time for the poor and less fortunate than himself, which probably meant that his own family were well off.

His skills as a herbalist must have been nurtured and helped along by some local healer. Perhaps in his dealing with the poor he came in contact with others who had skills he took to. As is often the case, it appears that the student soon outstripped his tutor for it was Fiachra who became famous for his knowledge of herbal lore.

Fiachra never got 'above himself' as they say. He worked tirelessly and helped wherever he could. He was a great man to have with you working the land, for his understanding of nature and its foibles were well known. It makes me wonder if perhaps he had come under the influence of the druidic teaching at some stage before he discovered the One True God. We have no way of knowing now so I may continue my story.

Even though it would have suited him very well to stay in one place and live a life of peaceful meditation and prayer it appears that, like all the saints of that time, Fiachra did a bit of moving about. Near the village of Graig na Manach (Village of the Monks) he founded an early Christian Church in a place called Ullard.

Young men flocked to join him in his work wherever he went and he did his best to teach them what he knew but they too were expected to pick up the spade and do manual labour in the gardens. He was a believer in self-support. Wouldn't he be a grand man to have around now?

Although he never turned anyone away, as far as is known, he did get weary of being in demand constantly and longed for a quiet place where he could just pray and be himself with his God.

Eventually he found such a place not too far away. It was a sheltered spot on the banks of the River Nore, where a well of spring water made it ideal. The River Nore flowed down through Ossory not too many miles away across country from the River Barrow where Graiguenamanagh was situated.

There was a nice stretch of pastureland bordered by a sheltering wood. It was everything a man like Fiachra could want. His retreat to this peaceful place must have given him space to do what he had always dreamed of. Working with the land, making his vegetable plot, growing and collecting herbs and it is likely that in his bid for self-sufficiency he had hives for bees. His days were filled with prayer as each task he set his hand to he did with a thankful heart. It is likely that in the evening time he would have a time for fishing in the river and watched the same sun set in the west as many a lad still does to this very day.

I always think that there is something timeless about a lad sitting fishing in the evening.

Poor innocent man, Fiachra thought he had finally found his own slice of heaven only to find, to his great consternation, that his followers had once again found him out and soon there was a well-trodden path to his idyllic retreat. He found himself drawn back into the everyday demands for healing and wisdom as word spread regarding his whereabouts.

I think he probably did as any of us would do. He went along with it at first but soon realised that there would be no peace at all for his own meditations, so he had to make a change. I have often wondered about life at that time for the saints in Ireland seemed to be over and back to Europe at the drop of a hat.

Fiachra was no different, he headed for France. When he got there he sought help from St Faro the Bishop of Meaux, who must have been known to him. St Faro granted him a small portion of land

so that he could have a place of his own. Maybe the poor bishop thought it would keep Fiachra out of the way.

There is a legend which says that St Faro told Fiachra that he could have as much land as he could entrench in one day with a furrow. A furrow is a drill where the earth is turned back on itself. Well, it was obvious that St Fiachra had no plough so it was probably expected that he would not manage to dig much of a distance by himself. But the story goes that St Fiachra set his staff to the earth and, moving along, made a great furrow where trees were toppled and rocks and undergrowth were turned out of his path.

Now, this is the part I was going to tell you earlier, where a woman came on the scene and, seeing what was happening, she ran to tell St Faro that Fiachra was not as holy as they thought as he seemed to be practicing witchcraft. St Faro realised that his strategy had not fooled God and that His blessing was with the Irish saint. So whatever Fiachra undertook after that had the support of St Faro.

In the quiet of that evening perhaps he told Fiachra how the woman thought he was practicing witchcraft, for from then on St Fiachra had no place for women near his monastery. He did this with the stipulation that if a woman disrespected this wish that she might expect to suffer pain from a severe bodily infirmity. Wasn't that a terrible thing entirely for a holy man to say? I often wonder about the old saints.

Well, even though St Fiachra went to France supposedly to find a peaceful retreat within a short while he launched himself into one project after another. Maybe he was trying to make up for his ill-wishing of the women. Who knows?

The first thing he did when he cleared the land, he had obtained, was to build an oratory dedicated to the Blessed Virgin Mary. His next move was only what you would expect from the saint. He organised a garden. This was a place of quiet contemplation as well as being part of the self-sufficiency policy Fiachra had always employed and instilled in his followers.

Perhaps his biggest work was the provision of a hospice where pilgrims could stay. Even with all this work going on he was busy instructing people in gardening skills and managing the land in line with nature.

People came to him seeking prayers and intercession and sometimes just ordinary wisdom to help them on their own paths. I expect that many of the pilgrims who came to him were women and he must have dealt with them as kindly as he did any other.

St Fiachra lived a long life and his death was reported in the year 670, in France, far from his native land where he once sat quietly by the River Nore.

He was buried in Meaux and many dispute the actual date of his death. Here in Ireland it is celebrated (sometimes) on 1 September but on the continent it is usually the 11 August. The pattern in his honour lasts from 15 August until 8 September.

St Fiacre's Well is still visited regularly and it is an old tradition that anyone travelling by boat will take a small bottle of the water with them. St Fiachra is believed to have saved a man from Graiguenamanagh from a terrible storm at sea and brought the ship safe to shore.

There is another legend which tells that the people of the area went to pray at the holy well and asked St Fiachra to help them during the Tithe Wars, when their cattle were being seized. As the bailiffs began to drive off the cattle a great swarm of bees came and drove the cattle back to where they came from. It would be a foolish bailiff who would argue with a swarm of bees.

Maybe these stories are true but sure, we have no proof, only word of mouth, handed down. The only thing we are certain of is that St Fiachra lived in the county and was a great man in his own time.

St Fiachra's Well is to be found at Sheastown outside Kilkenny on the road to Thomastown.

24

HOW KING'S RIVER
GOT ITS NAME

There are at least two versions of this story known to me and in telling the one most familiar I have to mention the second.

The second story says that Callan in County Kilkenny has no claim on the name of the ancient Ard Rí (High King) Niall Caille and that the River Callan near Armagh is the real location of his demise. While admitting to a discrepancy in the date of his death, AD 846, and the date given for his visit to Kilkenny, AD 844, I have a great leaning towards the Kilkenny version. Perhaps there is a third version where he survives Callan in County Kilkenny and meets his end in Armagh. Who can tell at this remove?

In the long ago time we had many kings in Ireland and I am not talking about the English kings who periodically sought to rule over us. We had a glorious time when not only had we kings, up and down the length and breadth of the land, but we had a High King (an Ard Rí). People are inclined to forget that now and think of medieval kings from across the water.

Well, the people of that grand town of Callan, to the south west of Kilkenny City, never forgot. The river, which sometimes flows gently and at other times in a flooding torrent, is called King's River (Abhann Rí). I have seen it myself in its deceptive mildness and have stayed well clear in time of flood. The flooding encroachment of that river through the townland would frighten the saints themselves.

The naming of the river goes back to a time when Ireland was under constant attack from Viking raiders. They were coming in all around the coast and by the mid-800s had become brazen and confident, setting up settlements in our best sheltered harbours. Before this they had been satisfied with raiding monasteries and taking slaves and heading back home in triumph, but now they were aware of the good land, the vast forests of good timber and the animals which thrived on the sweet grass. It seemed to them like a good place to bring their families and settle. Wasn't it better than the frozen north from whence they came?

Well, naturally enough, the Irish of that time were no different than we are ourselves today. They were reluctant to hand over what was theirs by birth right. The High King of Ireland at that time was known as Niall Caille mac Áeda and he was a descendant of the famous Niall of the Nine Hostages. Even though he was heart-scalded himself with the attacks by the Vikings along the northern and eastern coast, he was not slow in coming to the aid of the King of Osraige, Cerball mac Dúnlainge, who had only recently bent the knee to him and the King of Munster, Feidlimid mac Cremthanin. Niall Caille took his responsibilities as High King of the whole of Ireland very seriously.

He was coming along at a fine trot it appears, probably accompanied by Osraige's Rí, Cerball, when they came to the river which now runs through the town of Callan. There was no proper bridge or anything like that in those times so the High King and his companions had to find a way to get across. The river was swollen and flooding the woodlands and wide pasturelands around it, but they were desperate to get across to repel the Vikings who were coming up from a settlement they had set up in Waterford.

The urgency of their High King must have been contagious, for one of his loyal servants decided to try for a place which would enable his king to cross in safety. Sure, to him, what was it? Only a little river and it flooding. They must have crossed many rivers in their time together. Ah but the poor servant had badly misjudged the ferocity of the deceptive little river. He urged his mount forward, despite the creature's obvious reluctance and coaxed him out into the place he thought the flow of the river to be easiest, but with a sudden surge the water took the legs from under his horse and he was quickly submerged in the heaving brownish flood. The servant managed to get free of the horse and was seen struggling wildly in the turbulence as he tried to reach the safety of the land.

Niall Caille was a true king and, seeing his faithful serving man caught in the flood, he abandoned all caution and sent his own horse plunging into the river in a vain attempt to save the drowning man. But the torrent was no respecter of kings and with another huge heave of water, which had gathered strength all the way down from the Slieveardagh Hills, the Ard Rí of Ireland, Niall Caille, was overcome by the force of nature and drowned at that place.

It was only right and proper then that the people of that area should name the river, King's River.

The Ard Rí is said to be buried at Killree, farther along the river near Kells.

The King's River seems to enjoy a good flood every so often but in its more benign moments and during some long hot summers, barely

remembered now, the river had along its banks places of enjoyment and entertainment for the men, women and children of the town. I have even been assured that a certain Bishop of Ossory once swam in the area known then as the Horsehole, which was the preserve of the religious fraternity, school teachers, bankers and their social equals.

However, I am also solemnly assured that the poor of the town swam in an area known then as The Paupers. This was divided into a safe area for young children, called Sandy Bottom for more reasons than one. Next was the Little Paupers where the older children swam and then the Big Paupers for the adults. Further along, giving much more privacy to the holy and influential swimmers, was the place called the Horsehole.

Many men and boys have taken fish from the river down through the centuries for the King's River is home to the finest trout and salmon. The fish which spawn in this river have already journeyed from the sea up the River Nore. Isn't it wonderful that the creatures know when they meet the mingling of the waters of the King's River, where it joins the River Nore above Thomastown, and they turn and head home to Callan so the king fish come back safely to the King's River.

25

BLESSED EDMUND IGNATIUS RICE

On a recent visit to Callan I was viewing the ruins of the Augustinian monastery when I was drawn to the nearby Holy Well. The well is enclosed by low walls on three sides and there is access at the fourth side. To be honest it didn't look like a place of great veneration so I spoke with a young woman and child who were coming across the green towards the well. I was assured that not only was it a Holy Well but that every child in Callan knew that if you went to the well and said the words 'Holy bubbles come up to me' then the bubbles would begin to pop up through the water.

I know you are thinking that this is because it is a spring well, but how do you know if the bubbles are still rising when you are not there? I go with the children of Callan on this one.

Well, as I walked away from the site I began to wonder if that most famous son of Callan, Blessed Edmund Ignatius Rice, ever stood where I had and called on the holy bubbles. Maybe he did, who knows. He certainly knew the Augustinian monastery which over-looks the Holy Well. I have been told also that when he was a child he received help with his education from one of the Augustinian friars, Patrick Grace, who was also known as the Brathirin Liath (little grey brother).

Walking the streets of Callan can still bring the past strongly to mind. The boys of the Rice family, and there were seven of them, and their two step-sisters, must have known these streets well. Their father was Robert Rice and he was married to Margaret Tierney who was a widow with two girls when she joined her life to his. They were tenant farmers. It appears that the 160 acres was originally their own property before the Penal Laws made it impossible for them to own land. However, by some strange chance, Robert Rice was able to lease it instead. Whoever watched kindly over the Rice family gave the children a real chance in life.

Once again they managed, against all the odds, to receive an education, when by law they were forbidden to have access to the basic skills of reading and writing. Some say that the children were educated by visiting 'hedge schoolmasters', while others tell how it was the friar, Patrick Grace, who facilitated this education in their own home. Perhaps it was a mixture of both.

Edmund was born on 1 June 1762 in Westcourt, Callan, in the county of Kilkenny. He was the fourth boy born to Robert and Margaret and they were further blessed in the years that followed with three more sons. Life can't have been easy in a household with nine children but it seems to have been as harmonious as could be. The farm had to be worked and although it must have been hard on Robert to pay rent for what was truly his own place it seems he just got on with life and did not waste time on negative thoughts.

Margaret was a good mother and her kind heart saw many poor people fed at her table in spite of the crowd of children. People were generous then and compassionate to each other as they faced their common enemies: British rule, hunger and destitution. Compared to many others living in the Callan area, at that time, the Rice family were well-to-do and respected for their generosity.

One by one the children found their own way into the wide world. The older boys were always destined to take over the farm but Edmund knew that he must make a life for himself away from the farm. As was often done, the extended family offered him an opportunity of employment. His Uncle Michael, who was a merchant, in Waterford City, took him on in his chandlery business at the age of seventeen.

Well, Edmund took to it like a duck to water, as they say. He enjoyed the challenge of organising goods and supplying the many sailing ships which berthed in the port of Waterford. He would have been familiar with the smells and sounds of the busy port and they seemed to be enough for him because he showed no inclination, as many lads did at that time, to sail off and discover new worlds.

He knew how to sail and, because of his status, could afford to indulge his rowing skills as many young men did in those times. Being of farming stock he was always able to ride a horse and got great enjoyment from this activity. He lived a happy and carefree time despite the constant presence of the British soldiers. His work was useful and important so he did have a certain privileged status. His social activities were as any other young gallant at the time. He enjoyed dancing and all the frivolity that went with it. It was no wonder then that he finally became enamoured of a lovely young lady called Mary Elliott.

He was twenty-three when he married Mary and his joy was unconfined. Mary was the apple of his eye and they went everywhere together, she being as fond of outdoor activities as he was. His own people must have been very happy for him and probably his mother felt content that he now had someone to watch out for him. Ah, but it never pays to become complacent about anything.

His lovely wife Mary, after a year or two, became pregnant and they were absolutely delighted. Life was looking good and he was now an equal partner in his uncle's chandlery business. The only means of transport then was by horse and trap or on horseback. The gentry, of course, used horse-drawn carriages. They were both fond of horse riding and apparently, it didn't cross their minds that there was any danger when they rode out one day and she becoming heavier with child. There are no details except that she fell from the horse and sustained terrible injuries. The injuries brought on the early birthing of their little daughter, who would also be called Mary, and between one thing and another fever came on his lovely wife and she passed away shortly afterwards.

The loss of his beautiful companion must have been heart-breaking but he had a little daughter to care for so there were things to be attended to. His family and friends rallied round him but he was, for a time, inconsolable. His step-sister Joan Murphy came to live with him and take care of the little baby. He went through the same steps of bereavement as any of us do in times of great loss. He learned to accept the help people offered but sometimes he was glad to lose himself in work and other times he did not want anyone near him at all. In time he got through the first awful wildness of sorrow and was brought up short again when Joan broke the news to him that little Mary was not coming along as she should, and on further investigation they found that the poor child would be an invalid for her life.

Edmund had hit rock bottom now and it took every ounce of courage he could find within himself to go on. There is a time in sorrow when things reach a certain type of calm, like in the eye of a storm. Edmund hung on until that happened then he made arrangements for the future care of little Mary and turned to a life of greater spirituality. There was no question of him finding another wife but he became much more compassionate towards the helpless and poor children he saw around him in the streets of Waterford. The kindness he had experienced at his mother's table and her great example as she shared her food with the poor of Callan surfaced strongly now in Edmund.

He made it his business to know when people were in difficulties and did his best to help them get back on their feet again. He was known in the city jail and was often there to accompany prisoners on their last journey to the gallows. This was a far cry from the carefree lad who had stepped lightly through the streets of Callan.

Sometimes it seemed that Edmund would nearly burst with compassion he was so taken up with improving the lives of the poor around him. His fellow merchants asked him to go on the charitable boards operating in the city.

His brother John went to Rome to join the Augustinian Order and Edmund now found himself frequently thinking that perhaps that was a life that would be best for him. He was still running the business with his uncle but the desire to lead a more spiritual life was growing stronger and stronger. He gave himself no rest between business, charitable acts and prayer.

In his confusion he turned for advice to a motherly woman who had often helped him before. He told her his mind about joining an order and going to Rome. Her reply to him is reported as follows

'Well, Mister Rice, while you go and bury yourself in a monastery, what will happen to these poor boys? Can't you do something for them? Perhaps something similar to what Nano Nagle's Presentation Sisters have done in Cork?'

A lesser man might have ignored her words and gone on his solitary journey to Rome, but Edmund recognised the 'call' in her words and began to give real thought to what was needed by the children of Waterford and how he could improve their lot.

His uncle retired and left the business to Edmund in 1794 and for a few years he struggled to find the right path. In the meantime he realised that the young boys who lived in the streets around him had no educational opportunities and, despite the Penal Laws still being the law of the land, he began to work with small groups of lads, trying to give them some skills.

Then the time came when he saw his way clearly. He sold his business and began working towards the establishment of a school, and always at the back of his mind was the possibility that he could found a religious order. He knew all about the Augustinian Order and must have talked with his brother and his old mentor, Friar Grace of Callan, but the strictures of that order seemed too limiting to him and what he understood he must do.

Didn't he set up a little school in New Street in Waterford. The place was an old stable, but it was warm, dry and central to the core of the city. I wonder, did it cross his mind that Jesus started his earthly life in a stable? Maybe it did.

He employed two people to help him teach the boys who came to the school. But it appears that the lads who came were more than likely only interested in the shelter and warmth for they gave their teachers such a hard time that no money Edmund offered them would induce them to stay. This was a setback he had not expected. You cannot give to someone who does not want to receive.

He considered all sides of the matter and was coming to the conclusion that he was not suited to this path when two young men from Callan turned up at the school. They were Thomas Grosvenor and Patrick Finn. His brother, John the Friar, had sent them to him as they were expressing the desire for a spiritual life. His heart must have lifted with joy when they offered to join him in his work. They talked long and hard and it came to them that the boys they were trying to teach were not really bad or un-teachable but they were hungry and cold. That realisation was the turning point.

Edmund still had funds and they pressed ahead with the building of a small school on the hill which overlooked the city. They prayed and worked together and eventually decided that they would try and set up a religious order similar to that which the holy woman, Nano Nagle, had recently set up in Cork. She had founded the Presentation Order where the sisters went out and worked among the people, teaching and helping wherever they could.

The restrictions of the Penal Laws were easing and Waterford seemed to fare better in this respect because it was a busy port, and with so many coming and going it was almost as though the authorities ignored what was happening right under their noses in their bid to subdue the rest of the hinterland.

With support from Bishop Hussey and the guidance of Fr John Power they set out the plan for their Religious Order and it was sent to Rome for approval by the Pope.

Well, everything seemed to be happening at once now and Edmund was busier than he had ever been. The new school was built and there was accommodation for himself and his companions above the schoolrooms. To deal with the problem of hunger and cold he employed a woman to make clothing for the boys and a baker to make bread. So before they started lessons the boys were given fresh baked bread and milk and those in need of clothing found themselves measured and fitted in no time at all. With hunger and cold no longer tormenting the children, schooling could then be carried on.

The school was blessed by Bishop Hussey and it is said that he asked Edmund what the school would be called and Edmund replied that he would leave the naming to the bishop. The bishop is then reported to have looked out over the city and, realising that they were quite high above it, declared that Mount Sion would be a fitting name and so it has remained to this day.

The holy man from Callan drew men to him who wanted to lead a life of spirituality and service. It was not always easy and there were many obstacles on his path but the Presentation Brothers, as they were first called, and later the Congregation of Christian Brothers, were responsible for the education of many and their schools were a beacon to those in need in the early days.

Edmund lived a long and busy life until he became crippled with arthritis in the last years of his life. He passed away on 29 August 1884 and the people of Waterford mourned openly in the streets.

He is now buried in Edmund Rice Chapel, Mount Sion, Waterford. He was beatified in Rome in October 1997. Blessed Edmund Rice is credited in 1976 with a miraculous healing of a young man, Kevin Ellison from Newry. The medical profession said there was no hope for him and he would be dead within 48 hours but a relic of Blessed Edmund was placed on him and he made a miraculous and unexplained recovery.

In order for Blessed Edmund Ignatius Rice to be raised to saint-hood more miracles are required by the Vatican. My own thought on this is that miracles are relative. To children hungry and cold it was a miracle to be fed and clothed. To families who had no hope of education and then suddenly it is provided, that was a miracle. To the condemned, faced with the gallows, a compassionate man to walk beside them on their last journey was a miracle.

In the minds of the people of Kilkenny and Waterford the good man from Callan is already a saint and his own people, in the town of Callan, have raised a beautiful memorial in Green Street. The home where he grew up has been preserved and it is possible to visit it should you pass that way.

The feast day of Blessed Edmund Ignatius Rice is on 5 May.

26

The Rose of Mooncoin

If you have ever stood in Croke Park, or indeed in any hurling pitch, in County Kilkenny or elsewhere, when a Kilkenny hurling team took to the field, you will understand what I mean when I say that this lovely ballad has huge power. Once the first chords of the 'Rose of Mooncoin' are played, the whole attendance seems to gel and become one. Even the supporters of the opposing teams find it hard to resist.

The story of how this ballad came into being is simple and easy to understand and I will tell it to you the way I know it.

A long time ago, when Ireland was occupied, many good and bad things happened. One of the good things, which swung in that balance, was that there was an education available even in the small village of Mooncoin. Granted, it rested with the whim of the English Crown. Sometimes the Irish were permitted to have schooling and sometimes it was prohibited under pain of death. Imagine that state of affairs.

The time I am telling you about was just after one such prolonged banning of schools, and brave people were beginning to teach children openly. One of the terrible things happening at that same time was that the 'Tithe Act' was still being enforced.

Under the Tithe Act all the local people were bound by law to pay tithes or dues to the local Protestant clergy. People were very poor and some of the tithes demanded were absolutely destroying those who had little or nothing to live on already. So there was a lot of unease in almost every corner of the country, let alone in County Kilkenny.

This is how things fell out in Mooncoin. A man called Henry Murphy moved into the area in or around 1800. How he came there is not recorded, but he must have been a good man for he set up a school nearby in Carrigeen (little rock). He was the principal there for a good long while and his son, who was called Watt, which was probably short for Watty or Walter, decided to start up another school in the village of Mooncoin. I am told that it was in Chapel Street near the halfway mark, but I have no way of knowing now, no more than anyone else.

To return to my story, Watt was a scholarly man and given to writing the odd piece of poetry. Indeed, he followed the path of the bards of old who could wither a man with satire.

Now, Watt was well aware of the hardships suffered by the locals under the demands of the Tithe Act, and nothing would do him only to put his pen to paper. Didn't he write a blistering poem about the landlords, they being the ones who enforced the law.

If we had the words of it today wouldn't we use them, and we to be pitied with the impositions being made on ourselves.

The poem was read far and wide and, while some saw the justice in it, others took it very personally indeed, and the upshot of it all was that Watt was severely taken to task and his meagre wage, as principal of his little school in Chapel Street, was stopped forthwith. You see, his school was under the patronage of the Church, as were many other small schools just started at that time, and upsetting the gentry was not something they could support.

The position of the Church itself was precarious, with Catholic Emancipation finally granted, against much opposition, and written into law in 1829. The last thing they needed was for a school under their patronage to be seen as a hotbed of anti-establishment activity. Bless us and save us, couldn't young Watt, the schoolmaster, be turning out rebels under their very noses?

It must have been very difficult for him to survive, but I think he had great support from the locals. Nor indeed did he take the lesson to heart, for his pen was never far from paper, and it seems he was the author of a piece of prose about the Battle of Carrickshock also, and so became known as 'The Rebel Poet'.

Time was moving on for Watt and he was not yet married. He had a little house in Polerone, not too far away, down near the banks of the River Suir. Watt was a scholarly man and liked nothing more than to engage in debate, so when a new neighbour moved in nearby he was pleased to find it was a man of the cloth with a good education.

His new neighbour moved into the rector's house, which was located beside Polerone Church. In spite of his previous denuncia- tion of the Tithe Act, he became very friendly with the neighbours and in particular he got on very well with the daughter of the house, Elizabeth. To be honest he became infatuated with the beautiful Elizabeth, who was also fondly called Molly. Now she was almost thirty-six years his junior, he being around fifty-six and she only twenty years growing, as they say.

Sure, who are we to judge? She was well educated, and they had common interests, so it was often they would walk out along the banks of the river, talking and discussing this and that, reciting favourite poems, and occasionally writing them as well. Her father was not long in the district when he was made aware of Watt's poetic satire. Weren't some people tripping over themselves to tell him? Human nature is a strange thing entirely.

Elizabeth was, by all accounts, a handsome young lady, and there were many who would have wooed her if it were not for her apparent attachment to the rebel poet Watt Murphy. It was clear now to see that Watt and Elizabeth were more than fond of each other. Whether Watt approached her father with the request for her hand or not is not known, but there was a terrible disagreement, and even though Elizabeth loved Watt and didn't care about the age difference, her father would have none of it.

She was only twenty years old and so, by the old custom, was under his parental control. He moved swiftly, despite her pleas, and the assurances of Watt that he would love and care for her. Elizabeth was put on board a boat in the port of Waterford and sent to England in 1848.

Watt was left broken-hearted.

I know what you are thinking now, 'Couldn't he have followed her?' Times were different then, and where would poor

Watt get the money to follow her, even if he knew where she was gone. Also he would be in trouble as she was still under her father's protection, being only twenty.

Watt turned to the pen again. It was his only comfort now. He poured his heart into this beautiful ballad and called it 'The Rose of Mooncoin'.

How sweet 'tis to roam by the sunny Suir stream,
And hear the dove's coo 'neath the morning's sunbeam.
Where the thrush and the robin, their sweet notes combine,
On the banks of the Suir that flows down by Mooncoin.

Flow on, lovely river, flow gently along.
By your waters so sweet sounds the lark's merry song,
On your green banks I'll wander where first I did join
With you, lovely Molly, the Rose of Mooncoin.

Oh Molly, dear Molly, it breaks my fond heart,
To know that we two forever must part
But I'll think of you, Molly, while sun and moon shines
On the banks of the Suir that flows down by Mooncoin.

Then here's to the Suir with its valley so fair
As oft times we wandered in the cool morning air
Where the roses are blooming and lilies entwine
On the banks of the Suir that flows down by Mooncoin,

Flow on, lovely river, flow gently along
By your waters so sweet sounds the lark's merry song
On your green banks I wander where first I did join
With you, lovely Molly, the Rose of Mooncoin.

Watt took many a lonely walk by the banks of the River Suir, but never again was he to meet his darling Molly, the love of his life. Their companionship was of the rarest kind, and even in these enlightened times it would probably be frowned upon.

There is no information on what became of the lovely Elizabeth, whether she too mourned the loss of a precious friendship or went on to find a new love.

Broken-hearted Watt lingered in Polerone and passed away some ten years later. He was laid to rest nearby in Rathkieran cemetery.

This ballad has been adopted as the Kilkenny GAA anthem. It was a good choice given the wealth of emotion it stirs up in the manly hearts.

27

THE CARRICKSHOCK STORY

There are many and varied accounts of what is known as the Carrickshock Incident or The Battle of Carrickshock but to have any understanding of this event you need to know about the state of the country at that time.

It was a hard time for the people of Ireland and in particular the Catholic poor – and indeed the Presbyterian and the few Protestants who dared disagree with the establishment. You will have heard of the Penal Laws, I am sure, when you were going to school, and at that time you probably didn't pay much attention. The people who lived through them and died during their enforcement never had that luxury, God love them.

The only relief from the Penal Laws came with the much opposed Catholic Emancipation Act being introduced in 1829. It was a tenuous easing of cruel laws, the last of which was finally abolished in 1920. Imagine that. But in the meantime there was the Tithe Act to be contended with and it was a terrible burden on the poor people.

If you were a farmer or owned even a small plot of land you were expected to give one tenth of the value of your produce or pay 'in kind' to support the local Protestant clergy. I suppose it was bad enough that the invaders had taken over the country but to expect the poor people to pay them for the privilege was definitely a step too far.

It was a terrible time, a scandalous time when every liberty had been stripped from the native people. To say that they were downtrodden would be a huge understatement. Everything was taxed, even God's good light. So you could only have the windows you could afford to pay tax for in your little houseen. That is why some poor craturs only had one window in their homes and some none at all. Wasn't that an awful state to be in and the sky lit up with free daylight?

Well, that was how things were and they got worse in the year,1831. That year people were so far reduced that they found it impossible to feed themselves and pay their way, let alone pay tithes to an imposed clergy, they rebelled. Small blame to them as the man said.

They had just come through one of the hardest winters on record, in the previous year, 1830, and then the first months of 1831 were still snow-laden and bitterly cold. The people were without any help to tide them over the bad times.

To be fair to the people involved in this story, they came together in a delegation in the month of January, when snow still covered the ground. They approached Dr Hans Hamilton, who was the rector of Knocktopher and the surrounding smaller parishes, and tried to get him to lower the tithe as it was destroying them. He must have been a hard-hearted man for he not only refused to consider any reduction but he took legal proceedings to enforce the collection from the unfortunate people.

As in all legal matters this took time and it was the month of December by the time anything happened in south Kilkenny. Dr Hamilton must have had more than prayers on his mind, for he even had a land agent, a man by the name of James Bunbury. He must have been cute enough himself for once he was instructed by Dr Hamilton to serve the tithe processes on the miserable tenants, didn't he employ the local butcher, one Edmund Butler, to do the actual serving of the legal papers.

To my mind butchers are always men to be careful of, given their trade, you understand. Well, Edmund Butler was suited to his role and his local knowledge of who was who gave him an edge over any outsider who might have been sent in to do the serving of papers.

Butler was no fool either and he sought and received protection through the local resident magistrate, Joseph Green. It must have been a time of great fear in the ranks of the powerful for didn't Green authorise an escort of constabulary numbering thirty-eight and they all under the competent command of Captain James Gibbons, who was well used to military engagements having been, it is said, involved in the Napoleonic Wars. If it was in present times we would say he was overqualified for the task.

It was 12 December when they first set out, escorting bould Edmund, the butcher, as he delivered the legal papers, and they met with no resistance. People were probably shocked and it is likely that a lot of them were unable to read the words issued to them. Many had been denied education because of their religious leanings.

Edmund Butler, secure in the protective care of the constables, and probably feeling himself superior to these people, is said to have acted in an insulting and provocative manner when serving the papers. It was a dangerous attitude to adopt as he was soon to discover.

By the evening of the second day of process-serving, 13 December, an upswelling of anger brought together a large gathering from all the parishes of the people who were expected to pay tithes to Dr Hamilton. Many outraged sympathisers joined them. What could they do? They had no legal means to fight back. They were, as the man said, 'slighted and benighted'. Amid much talk and raised voices and a dangerous new high of emotion some plan must have been made.

Later that evening William Keane, a man who was said to be a hedge schoolmaster, and was staying in Ballyhale, approached some members of the constabulary and warned them that if they continued their collecting the following day they could expect trouble. Whether he was a spokesman for the people who had gathered in anger or not I do not know but he had the education and would probably have been chosen to deliver the message.

The good man's warning had no effect and the next day saw the butcher, Edmund Butler, gaitch brazenly out among his neighbours, closely guarded by the constabulary. Wouldn't you wonder at him? He must have given no thought at all as to how his relationship with the community would be afterwards.

Well, before the morning sun had dried the grass the process-servers had good reason to be concerned about the local community, for the said group were now thronging into the area. There were groups in paramilitary formation following close behind them. The bells in the local chapels were being rung and it was not for the saying of the Angelus, let me tell you. A lot of church bells then were set up outside in the grounds and could be sounded by anyone so the Catholic clergy could not be blamed, though some would, no doubt, have been on the side of their flock.

As the crowd continued to swell, horns were sounded near and far, and it is very likely that by now Edmund Butler was sweating a little. The men escorting him must also have felt a growing unease. Sure, they would have been foolish if they were not concerned by this stage. It seems that the people were coming close on all sides of them and into the fields surrounding them by now.

It was almost lunchtime, not that anyone had any interest in food, when the party guarding Edmund Butler proceeded from Ballyhale district towards Hugginstown.

When you look back on it now it would appear that they were almost herded into this narrow boreen, with high stone walls, near Carrickshock and suddenly they found themselves unable to move forward or in any other direction.

If Edmund Butler had been sure of himself the previous two days he now had real reason to be afraid, for the cry went up from the huge crowd. They wanted Butler. He was the focus of all their hatred and anger. They knew in their hearts that they would be ground down by the superior force of the foreigners' law but they would have Butler.

They say that the call was 'We'll have Butler or blood'. 'Butler or blood.' You can hear the chanting of it in your mind as each voice took up the call and it rising like a war cry.

There is nothing as frightening as a throng of people, with combined intent, and with nothing left to lose.

Captain Gibbons must have realised from the moment they set out that day that things were going to go from bad to worse. He could have called it off immediately the people started to follow. There were many options open to him, as the day advanced, but he continued stubbornly on. Now, as my father used to say, he found himself rightly calfhookled. No way out.

He must have shouted, threatened, ordered, but it was to no avail, for out from the throng darted a young man, leppin' with bravery. They say he was named James Treacy. He grabbed a hold of Butler and tried to drag him into the roaring crowd. Butler was pulled from his grip and even in that tight press of bodies two constables managed to bayonet young Treacy and, reacting almost in the same breath, Captain Gibbons shot him.

At any other time the firing of the shot would have halted the crowd but there was a hail of stones in instant reply and Butler was struck on the head by a stone.

That was when Captain Gibbons ordered his men to open fire. Even though they were hard pressed, the men fired at least twenty rounds into the crowd but were unable to reload as it was a difficult manoeuvre with the length of the weapon and the danger of bayoneting their own comrades. By this time they were tightly packed together, with little or no opportunity to use the drills they had been taught. They were horrified to find that what was easy on a parade ground was impossible in the actual press of battle.

In furious response the crowd surged forward, tearing the stones from the walls at either side of the boreen, and inflicting mortal injuries on the cornered constables. Nor had they all come empty handed to the fray. Pikes and scythes were used as indeed were hurleys and batógs (stout sticks) and there has even been a mention of mallets being used by some. I suppose it was a case of whatever came to hand as they set out that morning.

It was vicious, vengeful and intense for a short while and when the blood began to cool and people realised the awfulness of what had just happened they began to withdraw. There is something in human nature that, having festered and burst, leaves one horrified to have been involved or carried along on the wave of darker emotions.

Among the dead, lying broken and destroyed, was Edmund Butler, the butcher, who would swagger up to a neighbour's door, in contempt, no more. Captain Gibbons was laid low as were eleven of his constables. Fourteen constables were severely injured and what befell the remaining thirteen who set out that morning has never been mentioned. Perhaps they were just less seriously wounded.

After young James Treacy was killed two more of the crowd also lost their lives. They have been named as Patrick Power and Thomas Phelan. The twenty shots which the constables got off before they were overrun must have done some damage but no one has ever said how many people were injured and I expect many injuries were hidden in the days and weeks which followed.

The Revd Hamilton must have feared for his own life when he saw the result of his heartless court action. Apparently he quickly gathered up his possessions and departed to the safety of England, under cover of dark the following night. He never returned to face the people he had treated so badly when they were in need, for he died some years later.

In the days and weeks that followed there were many arrests. Eleven men were taken to trial in Kilkenny early in the following year. The charge was murder.

The whole country was in upheaval. The Church of Ireland bishops came together in great alarm and suspended the collection of tithes.

Daniel O'Connell was on hand to defend the first of the men charged, John Kennedy. By a great stroke of luck a ballad had been composed by a rebel poet, about the battle at Carrickshock, and it was being sung on every street corner in the country. This was Daniel O'Connell's strongest card. He claimed that not only was it impossible to have an impartial jury but the ballad being sung was prejudicial to a fair trial. The trial of the rest of the men was postponed to July in the hope that things might have cooled down by then.

Four months later not only had matters not settled down but they were escalating again. The Tithe War was still simmering. Shortly before the court was again to sit and charge the remaining men, a huge crowd, some say it was more than 200,000 people, gathered in Ballyhale, from all the surrounding counties. It was called an anti-tithe meeting but the real purpose was to intimidate jurors who were called to sit for the murder trials.

The chosen jury were not foolish. There is nothing like having a hung jury to stem the flow of legality. Eventually all the charges were dropped and the eleven men went free.

On the evening of the acquittals bonfires lit the night sky in a line drawn from Wexford, along the banks of the River Suir and on into County Tipperary. Every mountain, hill and raised place bore beacons of triumph with flames leaping high into the night air.

However, in spite of all the protests throughout the country, the collection of tithes was resumed the following year and continued until 1838.

Note: Humphrey O'Sullivan in his diary of that time 'Cinnlae Amhlaóbh uí Súileabháin' *mentions how he could see in every direction the bonfires burning on that night.*

The poet Seamus Ó Cathail wrote about 'Carriag Seac' *and his work* 'Oíche na dTine Cnámh' *(Night of the Bonfires) is often quoted by people who speak about the Carrickshock Incident.*

There is a memorial to this event in Carrickshock, which was erected in 1925.

28

THE PRIEST HUNTER
FROM BISHOP'S HALL

In Penal times, which stretched from 1695 to approximately 1793, it became common for criminals facing the death sentence, under English Rule, to be offered a pardon in exchange for becoming a priest hunter. Given the option, many took the job.

Queen Anne, a Protestant, had no mercy on the Irish Roman Catholics who had not willingly changed over to Protestantism at her command. She had no objections when her supporters suggested another law to be added to the already crushing Penal Laws. The Penal Act of 1709 ruled that all Catholic priests must take the Oath of Abjuration and give the Queen due recognition as Head of the Church of England and Ireland.

To refuse to take this Oath would mean execution for treason.

With priests all over the country going into hiding the priest hunters came into the good times. Rewards were offered to them, much the same as to bounty hunters of the Wild West.

A Reward of £100 for the capture of an Archbishop.
A Reward of £50 for the capture of a Bishop.
A Reward of £20 for the capture of a priest and £10 for a hedge school teacher.

Wasn't that a terrible state of affairs? Men being hunted like animals and indeed sometimes with animals chasing them, for bloodhounds were used sometimes.

When we were young we often heard tales of how this house or that house had a priest hole or a secret room concealed within the building, where hunted priests could hide when they were in danger. It was common for many 'Big Houses' and large farms to have these secret places built in from earlier times, when warfare between clans or invaders, demanded sudden safe places.

Often our imaginations would run away with us and we would have nightmares about being caught by the dreaded priest hunters. Little did we know that we were at that time within, as they say, an ass's roar, of a place where a priest hunter once held power.

As we got older we heard about a man called Bishop, of Bishopshall, and many another tale about that place as well. Hauntings and the like were easy stories which we could believe or not, but the story of the priest hunter was different. The man's name was Bishop and I cannot tell you his first name, and he must have had one, but there were people bearing that name in Bishopshall from around 1749, and a George Bishop was there up to 1815, according to the old records.

The bishop of this story was not known for shepherding a flock. He was like the wolf preying on them. Being a priest hunter gave him power and he was not afraid to use it.

The people of the surrounding areas lived in constant fear. He was clever and cruel and nothing pleased him more than to capture a priest. He would then endeavour to extract information from the unfortunate prisoner about the people who sheltered him and where other priests might be found. He was fond of money, and catching priests brought rich pickings.

Echoes of dark deeds seem to linger in places, and Bishopshall always seemed to hold old resonances when we used to cycle up through Cappagh as children.

Now, to get back to my story, there were many priests being kept safe in different parishes by good people, and one of these was the parish priest of Glenmore and Slieverue. He was Fr Richard Cody. He was a good man and much loved by the people. He would go to a sick or dying person at great personal risk and said Mass out under God's sky in several different locations, all of which were kept secret and were mostly hidden from view. One such place was in Athnarelaun. It was a high place called a 'knock' locally. It had plenty of cover from furze bushes and scrub. Here, he and his flock would be relatively safe, and lookouts could see for miles around if there was any sign of redcoats or indeed priest hunters.

The people would gather, coming singly or in pairs, from different directions and then Fr Cody would say the forbidden Mass and give the Eucharist to the little gathering. Afterwards the people would slip away quietly through the fields and home to their own places.

It happened that Fr Cody came to the attention of Bishop, the priest hunter. The Lord only knows how Bishop got his information and we are probably better off not knowing.

Once Bishop got wind of Fr Cody's activities he was determined to catch him. It is said that he employed a fellow Protestant by the name of Kearney from a place called Kearney's Bay, to help him hunt down and capture Fr Cody.

Now Fr Cody was not a foolish man, by any means, and he was in the habit of sheltering in a different house each night. It was the done thing then for anyone on the 'run' to be taken in and kept safe for at least the night. One night he was due to stay in Aylwardstown House, in Glenmore, not far from where my own father was reared, and somehow Bishop found out.

He sent word to Kearney, who came across from Kearney's Bay, which bordered the townland of Aylwardstown, and he instructed him to surround Aylwardstown House and seize Fr Cody.

Bishop, for all his cleverness, never counted on human nature. Kearney might work for Bishop, now and then, but he never liked the man and hated his methods. Kearney also had to live in the next townland to the owners of Aylwardstown House, and was no fool.

By devious means Kearney sent word to Aylwardstown that Bishop had ordered the capture of Fr Cody that very night and that he knew he was to stay in that house. How he did this is unknown. Perhaps the message was passed on by the man walking in the fields, saluting a neighbour, or by the lad calling to collect a gallon of milk or by the girl bringing eggs to the Big House. All had the opportunity and perhaps under the very nose of the priest hunter's spy.

However he managed it, Kearney's warning enabled Fr Cody to evade capture.

When darkness fell the bould Kearney approached the house accompanied by Bishop's men. They surrounded it and gained entry to search. Never by a nod or wink did Kearney betray that he was aware that Fr Cody was long gone. They searched the house from top to bottom but found neither priest nor any sign a priest had ever been there. Not even a secret room.

Bishop was a very frustrated man that night and Kearney must have slept the sleep of the just.

Fr Richard Cody continued to minster to his flock and always evaded capture. He is reported to have died of natural causes.

In the following years the lives of priest hunters hung by a thread. The people were no longer willing to be hounded and wanted to take back control of their lives. Politically times were changing, and Catholic Emancipation was becoming a reality. By 1827 the priest hunters were out of work and many of them vanished away to England to start another life.

Whatever befell the priest hunter of Bishopshall I do not know, but I expect he took the road to Waterford and left by boat as soon as he could.

29

THE BRIDGE OF CLODAGH IN THE ROWER

There is a story told about The Rower, which sits between the River Nore and the River Barrow a little above where they meet. The Rower is famous for its strong hurling men, and the first time I ever heard it mentioned it was in connection with a hurling match where they were described as fierce opponents. But the story I want to pass on to you is just a light-hearted old tale about the Bridge of Clodagh. The bridge itself is very old, and the story comes from a time when there were no televisions or radios, and an amusing tale was most acceptable among the locals. Indeed, they often time tried to outdo each other with their flights of fancy.

Not far from the Bridge of Clodagh there is a small waterfall, and below this again there are some deep holes. These holes are known as 'Kerry holes'. You see, they say that these holes are bottomless, so woe-betide anyone who gets into trouble there.

Well, one time, many years ago, a local man decided to try and gauge how deep these holes were. It was his intention, apparently, to give the lie to the story that they were bottomless. He went and got for himself a terribly long rope, which in itself was a wonder to behold. In order to do the sounding properly he needed some good weights, so off he went to a place known as Allen's Mill where he borrowed four half-hundredweights which he duly attached to the rope. Wasn't the owner of that mill a trusting soul, God help him. But he was sure he would have his measuring weights back before the day was out. Anyway, no one could steal the weights as his name was branded on to them.

So, down everyone went to the place of the Kerry holes and, with the weights firmly attached and knots duly tested, they dropped them in what they deemed to be the deepest hole. Well, the rope played out rapidly, nearly taking the flesh from their hands, and then, with them still taking the strain, there was no more rope left to give out. They were struggling trying to hold on to the last biteen of rope when suddenly it gave way deep under the water and came flying back to them, minus the weights.

Oh *mile*, murder, the grand weights from Allen's Mill gone and lost forever into the bottomless hole. They had no scuba divers then, nor had they any notion that such a thing might exist in the future, so it was a chastened group who returned to confess that they had lost the good man's weights.

The story doesn't end there either for that same boyo was given transport to Australia some years after. It is told that he was walking on the beach in Sydney, and who could resist that same

place, with the heat baking down from the Australian sky, when lo and behold you, what did he stumble across only the missing half-hundredweights with a bit of rope still holding them together. He knew them immediately by the imprint of Allen's Mills on them.

'Well, now isn't that a strange thing?' said he. 'Our schoolmaster was right after all when he said that if those holes were bottomless that they would come out in Sydney in Australia because it is exactly opposite to the Clodagh Bridge.'

30

St Cainnech of Aghaboe (St Canice)

The name Cill Chainnigh (Kilkenny) is translated as Church of Cainnech so it is only fitting that St Canice, the name he ended up with, gets a mention in this collection of stories from the county. St Canice was the Latin for Cainnech and Latin was in use by all the learned and educated people when he was alive.

He was born in or around AD 515 or 516, in a place known as Glengiven in what is now known as the county of Londonderry. His given name was Cainnech moccu Dalánn. His father was a man called Lughadh Liathdhearg and he was of the Ui Dalainn tribe who once resided at Inis-Doimhle, which is known as Little Island in the River Suir. Lughadh was a bard and a learned man. Cainnech's mother was known as Maul or Mella and she seems to have been a very holy woman indeed for there is a church in Kilkenny known as Thompleamoul in her name.

Well, Cainnech couldn't help but be educated and holy with two parents such as he had and it seems that the lad thrived under their care. Eventually he was sent to study with St Finnian in Clonard in County Meath. The monastery in Clonard was famous throughout Christian Europe and many men journeyed far to obtain spiritual education there.

Cainnech became one of an elite group of students who were mentored by St Finnian and this group became known as the Twelve Apostles of Ireland. He and his companions were to become missionaries, spreading the Christian religion. St Colmcille became a close friend of Cainnech and they both had a love of literature. Cainnech took on the huge task of writing a commentary on the Gospels. It took him a long time and became known as '*Glas-Choinnigh*' or The Chain of Cainnech.

He journeyed far and wide from his native home and spent a lot of time in Scotland with St Colmcille, who was known as St Columba over there. The Scots are as bad as the Irish when it comes to changing names, Cainnech was called St Kenneth in Scotland, and helped establish many churches there.

There is a story told about how he went to the Island of Iona. The weather was very rough and the seas running high when St Columba reported to the abbot, St Adomnan that 'A certain holy and excellent man will arrive here among us before evening.' It seemed impossible that anyone could make a crossing from the mainland to Iona that day but before the evening was out Cainnech arrived safely and reported that his journey had been through smooth waters. This is one of the reasons that he is now known as the patron saint of the shipwrecked.

On his return to Ireland Cainnech went back to Meath and worked in what was then known as northern Osraighe. The local king, Coleman, gave him grants of land on which to build a monastery and part of this was known as 'The field of the Ox' or Aghaboe. He built a monastery there, which became very important and it was there he spent a lot of time working on his commentary on the Gospels. A story is told about how he often sought out quiet places in the woods so that he could work undisturbed. He would remain motionless as he worked on his writing and the deer would come and stay close by him even allowing him to rest his manuscript on their antlers. I wonder did this really happen. When I think what happened with St Declan and the deer obliging him by drawing his chariot, maybe it is in the nature of the creatures to help out the saints.

When Cainnech died in AD 599 he was buried at Aghaboe and his remains rested undisturbed there until the coming of the Normans in the twelfth century when the monastery was transferred into Kilkenny City. In the fourteenth century the town of Aghaboe was burnt and the shrine of Cainnech and his relics were lost in the fire.

The cathedral of St Canice in Kilkenny is built on the site of an old church dedicated to the saint. Many more churches in Ireland, Scotland and across the world as far away as Australia and New Zealand are dedicated to St Canice.

Another story is told about the Well of St Canice which is still accessible in Kilkenny City. The water from this well is said to be very good to take with you if you are journeying by sea. It is also said to cure ulcers and other ailments.

The feast day of St Canice is celebrated on 11 October.

31

TALES FROM JAMES STEPHEN'S BARRACKS

'The Barracks,' as it is referred to locally, has been part of the life of Kilkenny people for a long, long time. Some of the stories that are associated with it are of hard times, when Ireland was under occupation. But even then some who wore the uniform and marched through the streets and towns were our own people. The Barracks stood for many things but it always gave employment in the City of Kilkenny.

There were times when military bands played to entertain the local people and sporting events raised their spirits. But there were times when the tramp of army boots brought alarm. The Military Barracks has survived rebellion and insurrection, and today is proud of its military presence, the 3rd Infantry Battalion of the Irish Defence Force. Sons and daughters now enlist and are respected in their peace-keeping efforts all over the world.

James Stephens Military Barracks was named in 1969 after the founder of The Fenians. It is not the original barracks which kept order in Kilkenny in the pre-1798 Rebellion times. That small barracks, I am told, was situated on the site the Evan's Home now occupies. The lane beside it that leads to John Street is called Barrack's Lane to this day.

In the early days of occupation this barracks often resounded with the smart clip clop of the horses ridden by the resident cavalry. A troop of cavalry was part of the makeup of any garrison at that time. The Kilkenny Militia were resident here in the late 1700s. The Royal Irish Regiment knew the streets of Kilkenny as well as the battlefields of France, Spain and America in their early days. Later they must often have longed to taste a salmon fresh from the River Nore, or to hear a bawdy song from a Kilkenny tavern as they lay in the muddy killing fields of Europe during the First World War.

The world of the soldiers who passed though these barracks was filled with names of far flung places. They were shipped out to wars on the far side of the world, China, Burma, India, New Zealand and Egypt. The fortunate ones came home and in the late nineteenth-century it was often they would tell a yarn or two about how they were away fighting the Boers, the Dutch settlers in South Africa.

Many Kilkenny people will know the story about the dog called Lion, who was the mascot for the men of the 24th Regiment of Foot who were stationed in Kilkenny Barracks in the late 1800s. That animal accompanied the regiment when it sailed to South Africa to fight in the Zulu Wars. A memorial in the barracks bears the inscription 'Here lies Lion, the Regimental Dog 1st Bn. 24th Regiment, who died October 1884. The faithful creature followed the fortunes of the Battalion through the Kafir and Zulu Wars of 1877–79 and was severely wounded at the battle of Isandalwana.'

Lion must have survived his wounds and the long journey home because he spent the last years of his life at home in his native Kilkenny.

The First World War claimed its own victims from Kilkenny. Among those lost, heroic men was Captain James Arnold Smithwick, whose family came from Archer Street, Kilkenny. His father was John Francis Smithwick, MP, a merchant and Justice of the Peace. His mother was Marion, formerly a Power from Eastlands in County Waterford. He had a younger brother Richard and it was to these he bade farewell when he left Shanbally, County Cork and boarded the ship on 7 October 1914, which would take him to the front.

October weather at sea is fitful and the crossing in a packed sailing vessel must have been uncomfortable but not half as bad as what was to come. Thrust into the forefront of the battle with his regiment, he found himself leading his men, in atrocious conditions, at a place called Le Pelly, on 20 October. Although it was little more than a week since they had set foot in Europe they were already exhausted from lack of sleep and it must have seemed like a lifetime since they left Ireland.

According to a letter, which he sent to his brother Richard, afterwards, they found that they were being fired upon from a position to the rear of them and as he endeavoured to deal with this threat he was severely wounded and lay unconscious for a long time. After the battle had passed he was taken by a German ambulance crew, who noticed that he was alive, and they lodged him in an internment camp at Crefeld, where he was to spend the next ten months.

Eventually Captain James found that he was to be part of a prisoner exchange and was returned to London. The wounds he had sustained were still not healed and he was sent to Wandsworth Military Hospital, where he was visited by His Majesty King George V. It was a nice thing for the monarch to do and I am sure that James felt honoured by the gesture.

As soon as word came to his home in Kilkenny, that he was safe in London, his brother Richard quickly came to him. Richard must have been distracted when he saw how poorly his brother was. He did everything he could to ease his brother's suffering, making sure he had the very best of care, and spending long hours by his side.

It soon became evident that he was, as a result of his wounds, now suffering from the dreaded Consumption. He was transferred to Pinewood Sanatorium and eventually to a private nursing home. The gallant young officer who loved to play a game of golf or cricket in the quiet Kilkenny countryside lost his last battle and passed away a year later, on 12 November 1915.

He is laid to rest in Foulkstown, Graveyard in Kilkenny.

Another Kilkenny soldier who lost his life in that year was Private Daniel Deevy who came from Castlecomer. He was captured and held at a POW Camp in Lindberg where he subsequently died from his wounds. The date of his death is given as 30 April 1915. He is laid to rest in Foulkstown, Graveyard in Kilkenny.

You might wonder why I have told you about these two particular men when so many from county Kilkenny died in similar circumstances. The answer is simple. I have seen both men's Memorial Medallions recently, when Lieutenant Larry Scallan, curator of the Visitors Centre in James Stephen's Military Barracks, gave me the grand tour of this treasure trove of military history. He showed me the Memorial Plaques, as they were originally called, and explained how they came into being.

DEAD MAN'S PENNY
(A MEMORIAL PLAQUE OR MEDALLION)

The practice of placing coins on the closed eyes of a dead person was surely manipulated out of all proportion during the First World War. A widow or widower could expect to receive, by post, a large bronze medallion, five inches in diameter, which looked like a giant penny. This was officially called a Memorial Plaque or medallion but to the bereaved it became known as Dead Man's Penny.

It appears that the British Government became aware of the bleakness of their death notifications to the huge numbers of families during the early years of this conflict and decided to try to do better. The practice of sending out a few brief words stuck on a scrap of paper declaring someone 'LOST IN ACTION' in the shape of a telegram from the War Office was so final and awful that even their hard hearts were moved. Perhaps a close relative of someone in power had been lost to the war before the realisation dawned on them. A flimsy bit of paper announcing that their loved one had lost their life in the service of King and Country was no longer enough.

It was two years into the First World War before a Government Committee was set up to find a design for a Memorial Plaque, which would be sent out to the grieving relatives. The Committee must have realised that they did not have the expertise themselves to do a proper commemorative design so they did the next best thing. They decided to hold a competition. They first figured out what they could afford and then the size and weight of the proposed medallion. They debated the problem from November 1916 until August 1917, when they placed a notice in *The Times* of the competition and invited submissions from the military and general public. It was to be designed in a mould of wax or plaster and to comply with certain specifications.

Under the directions, an inscription, 'He died for Freedom and Honour' had to be included. In their innocence or arrogance they never thought that it might read 'She died for Freedom and Honour'. Later they had to scrunch up the letter H so that they could incorporate 'S' for She, as 600 or more women also lost their lives during this 'War to end Wars'.

The result appeared in *The Times* in March 1918. A design by the sculptor and medallist, Edward Carter Preston, called Pyramus, received the first prize of £250, which was a huge amount of money in those times.

After the war some of these bronze plaques were made in the same factories which had made the weapons of war. The War Office must have felt a bit more comfortable sending out these Memorial Plaques, which bore the name of each deceased on a raised rectangular section. No rank was included for anyone as all had made the ultimate sacrifice. The image of Britannia holding out an oak wreath above the name and a lion standing below with dolphins leaping in the background is unusual, but no matter how grand it appears this medallion could never compensate families for their tragic loss.

They also began sending out a message from Buckingham Palace, which bore a copy of King George V's signature, which read 'I join my grateful people in sending you this memorial of a brave life given for others in the Great War. George R.I.'

The relatives also received a Next of Kin Memorial Scroll which read as follows:

> He whom this scroll commemorates was numbered among those who, at the call of King and Country, left all that was dear to them, endured hardness, faced danger and finally passed out of the sight of men by the path of duty and self-sacrifice, giving up their own lives that others might live in freedom.
>
> Let those who come after see to it that his name be not forgotten.

We took a long time in Ireland to give due honour to our own fallen in wars away from home. Today our men and women still go out to countries most of us will never see and the names of places like The Congo, The Lebanon, Chad, Afghanistan and Syria will fade in local memory, but under the watchful eye of the military curator in the Visitor's Centre, we will remember them.

THE HURLING STORY

In the same military centre I was delighted to find a more modern section which contained winning medals for All Ireland Hurling and Camogie earned by members of the 3rd Battalion of the Irish Defence Forces who now occupy the barracks. Isn't it wonderful that life has turned completely around in Kilkenny since the cruel Statutes of Kilkenny which forbade the playing of hurling or any other Irish game? The Statutes further declared that the commoners should accustom themselves to use and throw lances, and other gentle games which pertained to arms.

Were they mad or what? A Kilkenny man or woman with a hurley was dangerous enough but to suggest that they learn to throw lances was downright daft. Wasn't it an awful pity the Kilkenny residents didn't take up the idea; Ireland would have been free much sooner. The result of this suppression of the honest game of hurling brought much misery and harm not only to the Irish but to the Anglo-Norman young men who had become adept at the game.

There is a story told of one young gentleman, Geoffrey FitzThomas, who was caught playing the game and was found guilty of the nefarious and detestable crime of striking a ball with a stick in the manner peculiar to the Irish. Oh it is easy to laugh now and we safe by several hundred years. However, for the young gentleman the guilty verdict was but the start of his troubles.

In the days that followed his arrest he was tortured and beaten as the authorities endeavoured to get him to name his fellow hurlers. Sure, the poor lad probably didn't know the half of them and even if he did he probably would have known them by a nickname only. As you and I know, we have always been a great nation for applying appropriate nicknames It is said he was subjected to stretching on the rack and 'dancing' on hot coals but he would not or could not name anyone.

Eventually, a much taller young gentleman promised the judge not to take up a hurl again. He must have been a bit light headed, after all that he had gone through for he foolishly declared that he just couldn't help himself when he saw the great skill of the lads playing hurling in the fields, as he rode by, and he had fallen under the spell of the strange foreign game. Ah, yes. Well, the judge sentenced him to forty lashes and two years' imprisonment with hard labour and said he would have him had sent to the gallows if the law allowed. After that the familiar description, in hurling, of bending, lifting, striking had a different meaning entirely for that poor devil.

Remembering that story and to see the medals and the names of their owners proudly displayed in the home of the military establishment was as they say 'a sight for sore eyes'.

KICKBOXING WORLD CHAMPION

A folk tale of the future concerns another soldier currently in the Barracks. My father, God be good to him, would laugh at this for the soldier bears a grand Kilkenny name, Vinny Di Ruscio. Vinny's story is the stuff of legends. He trained since he was a young in the art of kickboxing and finally in 2012 he won the coveted title of Kickboxing Middleweight Champion of the World when he beat the English fighter Zuccala.

MEMORIES

A story attached to one of the artefacts held in this collection fascinated me. At some time during the year 1917, in the middle of the war, some of the soldiers must have had a little time to rest and during those times they worked on little projects of their own, using whatever came to hand. Men who had different trades before joining the army still liked to practise their skills.

A soldier named Private John Dunne from Assumption Place, Kilkenny and his friends melted down whatever spare lead they could find and from that they had fashioned a cross. There was nothing unusual in that except that just before the molten lead became hard the three friends pressed their thumb prints into the back of the cross. The word Arras 1917 is written on it. God only knows what became of the three comrades before the war ended.

DE VALERA AND PETER'S KEY

Included in this memorabilia I found an account of this famous key. Peter de Loughrey was the name of one of the men who shared Lincoln Jail with De Valera when he was imprisoned in England. A rough cast key was smuggled in to them, hidden in a loaf of bread, and de Loughrey, who had been a locksmith, was able to adjust it so that it opened the door for their escape.

The Metal Harvest

On display also was the gruesome 'metal harvest' which is the debris of war being ploughed up and thrown on to the headlands of the fields of Europe, especially France. Some of this, which includes earth-encrusted grenades has been gathered and brought to Kilkenny as a grim reminder that war is never really over while mines and grenades are still buried just inches below the farming land.

I gratefully acknowledge the help and information supplied by Lieutenant Larry Scallan who is the curator of the Visitors' Centre in James Stephen's Military Barracks, Kilkenny.

32

THE LAST FITZGERALD IN CLUAN CASTLE (CLONAMERY)

There is a story about Cluan Castle which often makes me wonder if animals really do haunt certain areas where they once lived.

In the late 1600s the man who was in charge in Cluan Castle was Edward Fitzgerald. He made the mistake of taking the side of King James II and subsequently forfeited his lands. Apparently he was one of the better landlords at that time and was known for his love of music and in particular he liked to play the harp. The harp would have been the clairseach or Irish Harp and, when played by a Master Harper it could raise the listener to the heights of bliss or break their hearts with a lament.

Even when this castle fell into ruin, locals would still point to the window where he used to sit and play his harp. It must be a grand gift to have.

It is hard for us to understand how things worked all that long ago but, as owner of large tracts of land, Edward had in his care many tenants and retainers and in time of strife he could call on them to support him, or whomsoever he followed, onto the field of battle. He had been raised to this way of life and had often taken his people far from the banks of the River Nore to fight against different foes. At one time he took them as far north as Meath and they were engaged in the Battle of the Boyne.

Behind all this soldiering he was a man with responsibilities and probably should have given more thought to his own business in Cluan. Life then was so different that we can only guess at the pressure he felt and it is likely that he had good people left behind to manage his estates.

Well, when he took off to join in the Battle of Aughrim, with his own men gathered around him he probably felt relatively safe and relaxed. Aughrim was to be a journey of a similar distance across country as he had previously undertaken, and he probably had that terrible failing which sometimes besets the young, he thought himself invincible.

Whatever he thought, the poor man, he always must have expected to come back to his own family.

The Battle at Aughrim was to go down in history as the last battle fought on behalf of an unworthy king. The Irish had been used as battle fodder in their mistaken trust in James II. In the heat of the battle Edward Fitzgerald came off his war-horse and engaged the enemy with his sword. His horse-boy was a young lad, green to the field of battle, and his task was to hold and have the horse ready for his Lordship at any point in the engagement with the enemy. The battle raged around him and he was at his level best holding the fine strong animal.

As you would expect, he was in due course separated a bit from his master and when the terrified lad realised that the battle was being lost he must have been in dread and terror. By all accounts Cromwell's mounted troopers were trained to advance in a boot to boot close formation and not to engage in individual pursuit unless given a command to do so. It must have been a terrifying spectacle to see the mounted enemy advance like a great killing machine across the field of battle.

Whether he heard his master call out to him, to bring the horse, or not, no one can say now for the noise on a field of battle is a terrifying thing. Can you imagine the shouts and challenges, the screams of the dying, the neighing of the frightened horses and over all this the clash of swords and the raucous calling of the ravens who followed the battles then.

The boy must have been terror struck and there to his hand was a means of escape from what he must have perceived to be certain death. The big war-horse strained and pulled against him and then perhaps, because he was only a lad, he could no longer see where his master was, he took the only option for him at that moment and leapt to the stirrup and into the saddle and away, away from the terror behind him.

With no war-horse to take him to safety, Edward Fitzgerald must have felt the first surge of real fear. The plunging hooves of the retreating army all mixed up with men running and the enemy troopers cutting through them, intent on slaughter would have been enough to break a stronger man. Edward was no weakling, but he was disadvantaged in that he still wore his boots and spurs. He never expected to be on foot at a moment of flight. Indeed he most likely never expected to be fleeing the battlefield in the first place.

Edward Fitzgerald was a man like any other and it is said that in the full retreat by the Irish, finding himself horseless, he ran with the rest to get away from the mounted foe. His attire marked him as an important enemy so he was a target from the word go. I expect it never occurred to him to cast off his finery as he ran so he could mingle

with the less notable, so having run for a time probably almost to a safe place, he was caught up by a mounted enemy and struck down, mortally wounded, by one of the Williamite troopers.

As the Williamite army swept through and on after the fleeing Irish two of his followers found Edward among the slain and it is said that they wept firstly for the loss of The Harper and then for their leader.

On the morning after the battle his war-horse was found standing outside the stable in Castle Cluan and it was only then that his family and retainers knew the battle had been lost and that they, themselves, were now in mortal danger from William of Orange and his followers. What became of the boy is not known except that there are several tales about how he brought the war-horse home and fled in great sorrow from the place which had been home to him.

I came upon this following ballad during my research and thought you might enjoy it.

There stood beside the winding Nore
A castle fair to see;
It was the home of the Geraldine,
And a gentle knight was he.

But now a hoary ruin it stands
Beside the winding Nore,
All lonely, and all desolate
A hundred years or more.

An' though its woods each year grow green
And the clear Nore flows on,
Yet Cluan's tower shall ever be
A ruin grey and lone.

Cluan's lord was a true knight –
He fell amid the slain,
The first in fight for his king's right,
On Aughrim's bloody plain.

Two summer nights scarcely past
Since that last fatal day,
When Cluan's lady mourning sat
For her good lord away.

Oh! heavily and wearily
She sits within her hall
And startles often as if she heard
Her good lord's wonted call.

She sits beside her baby boy
As quietly he sleeps,
And recks not of the woes for which
His tender parent weeps.

And now she listens eagerly,
For hark! there comes a sound
Of footsteps, and her anxious eye
Is looking all around.

The sound grows loud and nearer
Along the well-known track –
Can it be true that her good lord
Is well and safe come back?

'Ho varlets all! Wake ye in haste,
And on your lord await –
I hear the stamp of his good steed
Without the Castle gate.'

Thus did she speak in ecstasy,
And well did all obey,
And quickly did the gate unbar
Ere yet began the day.

Down came the lady Eleanor
All trembling for joy,
And brings to welcome back his sire,
Her sleeping infant boy.

But oh! it was a dismal sight
To see the good steed there,
When Cluan's lord had not come back
To greet his lady fair.

Oh! Is he a prisoner to his foes,
Or fallen in the fight?
Or why comes back his gallant steed
In such a woeful plight?

Why stands he thus impatiently
Without a curb or rein?
There's blood upon the saddle-bow
And foam upon the mane!

'Oh, woe is he!' the lady cried,
'Sure this must bode of ill!
'To see those ruddy drops of blood,
My very soul doth chill.'

In vain they looked, they searched in vain
Around both tower and tree
But the last lord of Cluan's Hall
They never more shall see.

One summer day of dread and doubt
Had scarcely passed away
When a youth rode up in fearful haste
With looks of wild dismay.

'Oh! noble youth wilt thou not bide
To speak one word to me –
What means this look of wild despair,
Or whither does't thou flee?

'I am the lady of this tower.
You may find shelter here –
For friend or foe, which e'er you be,
Thou shalt have nought to fear.'

'For friend or foe, which e'er I be,
With thee I cannot bide –
A woeful tale is mine to tell,
And one I fain would hide.

'Our rightful King has lost his crown –
And all our hopes lost we –
Nought now is ours, and the proud foe
Exults in victory.

'I saw thy lord fall by my side
Amidst a heap of slain,
While swiftly flew his gallant steed
Across the battle plain.'

Thus having said, he turn'd his rein
No more she heard him speak;
The tears were falling from her eyes,
And pallid grew her cheek.

And well might she both wail and weep
To leave her kin and home –
Her lovely tower to seize upon
The ruthless foe is come!

And though its woods each year grew green
And aye the Nore flows on,
Yet Cluan's tower shall ever be
A ruin grey and lone!

Before I found this story my daughter had a very strange experience one night coming from Kilkenny on to Carrick-on-Suir. At one point of the road she swore that as she drove a great horse with a flowing white mane galloped alongside her car for a long stretch of the road. She felt no fear and it was as though the horse was taking care of her. Then just as suddenly as he appeared he was gone. Perhaps the ghost of the gallant war-horse still gallops towards home.

33

THE GILLYGILLY MAN

Long ago, when we were in school in Ferrybank it was usual that once a year the school had a visit from a GillyGilly Man. I suppose in these times he would be called a magician. As far as I can trace back, there has always been an entertainer who fitted into the name-bracket of GillyGilly Man. He invariable carried himself with an air of mystery and intrigue. There was always something about him which set him apart from the general run of people; an eye patch, a limp, a wild appearance.

Children were drawn to him but scared at the same time. He could perform feats of trickery and amusement and it was when he rested from these antics that he seemed to attract the older people to him. That was when he made his money. The seat beside him was never warmed for long by any one person but many leaned close to hear his words and a coin would sometimes glint in the sun as it passed to his hand.

This story tells of such a person with the singular exception that there was nothing physically or mentally different about him unless you would consider monumental laziness such an ailment. He was bone idle and that is the truth of it.

Sean was a farmer's son but his birthing into such a station in life was surely a mistake, for he considered himself above the hard labour involved in farming. He was born not too far from that lovely high place called Listrolin or in ancient times the Fort of the Wren. He was given to daydreaming and could idle a week away just wondering about little or nothing. The pattern of the clouds passing over what we now call the Walsh Mountains was a constant source of distraction to him. The fact that his father lost patience with him many a time, and by turn berated the mother who bore him for gifting him with such a useless son, it was no great wonder that things turned out the way they did.

Although his mother was well able to hold her own against the hostile remarks, Sean felt as though his very existence was becoming a rebuke and after many a blow was struck and many harsh words uttered Sean decided he would seek his fortune in the gentle wide world.

He speculated that anywhere would be better than the farm where he ate and drank his fill of sweet buttermilk every day and slept warm and comfortable each night, because if the truth were told he really never noticed all these things which were provided for him by his aging parents. All this lad could think about was how very demanding and crossacklesome his father was, as he expected him to rise early and work all day around the farm.

Sean had seen first-hand, at the local markets, that GillyGilly men seemed to make a good living by entertaining the people in attendance and the ladies especially seemed to be eager to pass a coin across their palms. His observations lacked the intensity which would have revealed to him that on the passing of the coin the GillyGilly man also spoke softly to each one. Had he taken the time he would have realised that people were asking for and receiving advice or direction. Young ladies in particular were always anxious to find out if a handsome young swain was due to come into their lives. Mothers were anxious about childbirth or their children or household and in the evening time it was often an old man might buy a drink for the GillyGilly Man and in return get information about the coming weather or the state of the world in general.

Ah no, Sean never paid enough attention to other people at all but in his blissful ignorance he donned a cloak and procured an old floppy hat similar to what he had seen these men wear. A stout ash staff was the final addition to his garb and he was sure he was going to make his fortune.

Fairs and market gatherings in those days were usually located at crossroads outside the nearest town and common ground was always found nearby where the animals could be safely penned.

Sean's plan was to set up on the edge of the market and do a few simple tricks which he had mastered after much practice. The three tumblers with the hidden pebble was always a draw and he was fond of showing how he could balance anything on his nose, his favourite being a cone of lighted paper which scared the life out of the watchers. Indeed he had often scorched his eyebrows doing the same trick, when a breeze blew the flames to life faster than anticipated.

The first time a young woman came and placed a shining coin in his palm and stood expectantly waiting he thought it was for a word of gratitude and quickly thanked her. When she demanded if that was all he had to say, he got flustered and she snatched the coin back and flounced away. She quickly spread the word that this GillyGilly man was useless and no one came to cross his palm with as much as a farthing after that.

Sean travelled to every fair and gathering, up and down the county and was often put to flight by hostile young farmers wives who told him he should be ashamed to be standing begging and he in the whole of his health. He was also soundly thrashed by members of the official begging fraternity who were known at that time as Fakirs. His word for them was not as genteel at all. After that he tried to disguise himself and adopted a limp. It eventually dawned on him

that he was not doing as well as he thought he should and there was only a very small jingle in the hidden pocket of his cloak.

It was in the Market Square in Kilkenny just before Christmas that he noticed he was being followed. He shifted position several times, moving quickly between tents and stalls to a new location but she was always there just on the fringe of the crowd, watching. She was an old hag wrapped in a dark shawl against the weather and her face was hidden behind a screen of straggling black hair. She disturbed his concentration more than once and his new-grown beard got singed badly during his trickery.

Once he noticed her, she seemed to be everywhere he went. Every little village or local fair he attended, there she was standing, watching. She never seemed to do anything but the intensity of her gaze unsettled him. His life became a misery and he dreaded seeing her because in the back of his mind he blamed his misfortune on this persistent creature. She was surely a figure of doom and his end must be fast approaching. His trickery lost its appeal because of his dour and watchful manner and people began to avoid him. Other GillyGilly men were making in on his favourite haunts so he decided that he might as well be miserable back home in the Walsh Mountains of south Kilkenny, where at least he had food and shelter, instead of tramping the roads haunted by this old hag.

His decision made, he gathered his cloak about him and started for home. He had long ago realised that other GillyGilly men were doing a bit of fortune-telling to make their money, but he could not bring himself to make up as much as a white lie to fool another soul. So it was back to the home farm and daily toil under the lash of his father's tongue.

Hunger cramped in his belly as he walked but he could see Sliabh na mBan in the distance and was almost back to his own place. He knew there was a well of fresh spring water not far ahead and there he would stop and refresh himself and water would fill a gap inside him. With any luck there might even be an apple or bit of fruit left there as an offering to the spirit of the well. The evening was drawing in when he finally came in sight of the well and he gladly lifted his step towards it. Almost upon it, he caught a glimpse of movement in the shadows, by the well, and then he saw a woman bending forward to cup the water in her hands and bring it to her mouth and face. As she raised the water her shawl fell back from her head and shoulder and he drew a quick breath as he glimpsed her beauty. Then she drew the shawl up around her head again and hung forward her hair. When she turned he saw that it was the old hag. His breath went from him as his eyes met her glittering dark ones and time seemed to stand still.

The moon was high in the night sky when he remembered himself again. The old hag was seated beside him but his hand was clasped tightly around hers. 'Come with me,' she said. 'I can teach you what you need to know. I have more than enough to support us both. I have loved you from the first day I saw you. Come with me now.' Sean found that his mouth was dry and he was unable to take his eyes from her. She gently shook his hand and the shawl slipped away again from her raven dark hair exposing the whitest and most beautiful shoulder he had ever seen. A sudden breeze blew the dark hair away from her face and Sean knew that he was lost forever.

Pretend to be something you are not and you may get caught by someone who is not who they seem.

The glitter of her eyes spoke of another world and although he was within shouting distance of the Fort of the Wren he made no call. He turned his back on the high hills of home and went with her. Their lives together became easy and peaceful. He learned about many things and could tell the trouble that beset a person before they spoke a word. He could tell of the weather ahead, at a glance, and what herbs would heal any illness. They lived long past the time allotted to most men and journeyed among people who looked eagerly for their coming.

He was no longer known as a GillyGilly man but some now called him a Fairy Doctor. Maybe he was, maybe he wasn't. Who can know with GillyGilly men?

Who the lady was we will never know but she had a power which was not mortal and she used a mortal to do good. Her passing is not recorded except that the GillyGilly man lost all interest in life in this world once she was gone and spent his last days relating his story to any who would listen but always his gaze would seek the gentle slopes of Sliabh na m'Ban.

It seems that they lived together as long as was decent and died when they couldn't help it.

Printed in Great Britain
by Amazon

15478480R00111